HOMEWARD

The Mountain Man's Babies

FRANKIE LOVE

Frankie Love

HOMEWARD
The Mountain Man's Babies Book 8

Idaho is the last place a man like me would ever
expect to find the woman of his dreams.
But there she is, running a Bed & Breakfast,
with her heart-shaped face and magnetic smile.
And she has no idea who I am.
Just like me, there is more to Laila than meets
the eye—this girl has been broken more times
than she can count. She's lost all faith in a man
ever helping her piece together her shattered
dreams.
But she's never met a mountain man like me.
The distance between her heart and mine may
seem wide, but I refuse to give up because she

deserves happiness more than any woman I've
ever known.
I may be stuck in the middle of nowhere, but in
her arms, I feel like I've come home.

Dear Reader,

*HOMEWARD features hidden identities, secret
babies, and a few stalkers who aren't going to stop
until they take what they want.
Don't worry, no one is gonna mess with the babies on
Miracle Mountain, I can guarantee you that!
This story is steamy, sweet, and sure to make you want
to fall into the arms of the closest bearded-hottie.
Enjoy!
xo, frankie*

Chapter One

COLTON

I knew I needed to leave. That if I had to spend one more day dealing with Rozzy, and her brother Rick... I'd lose my shit. One date with Rozzy was all it took; now she thinks we're meant to be.

But I know she's meant to be out of my life.

Unable to shake either of them, I left L.A., knowing a long-ass road trip was one way to avoid the pair of gold-diggers. Sure, I could have gotten a restraining order--and maybe I should have--but I didn't want to get my name in any paper. I'd gotten so sick of the bullshit of this town over the past year that all I wanted to do is keep my head down--Rozzy was just the last straw.

Now, after driving for a month on a trip to clear my head, I'm lost.

Literally and figuratively, and I don't know if I'll ever find my way back home.

Do I even know where that is anymore?

I can't get a cell signal, and who would I call anyway? I don't want to talk to anyone in L.A. Not right now -- not until I absolutely have to. Which, according to my calendar, is in two days' time, when I'm supposed to step foot on the set of my new movie.

But that seems ages away right now. Maybe because I have no fucking clue how I'm gonna get from here to there. Doesn't help that I don't even know where *here* is.

The air conditioning is busted--and a few months ago, that fact would have grated on me. Back then, if anything didn't go my way, I'd pay to get what I want.

But I didn't like the man I'd become.

So, when I got word that the movie was shooting in the middle of nowhere, Washington State, I knew I needed to take a long-ass drive and spend some time figuring my shit out.

Now, with the windows down, the wind rustling through my hair, a hand running over the thick beard I've been growing for this movie, I feel myself relax. The sun may be beating down on me, but I'm feeling alive for the first time in years.

This fresh mountain air is good for the goddamn soul, I figure.

But getting lost in the mountains of Idaho when the sun is starting to set? Not so much.

After driving a few hours through miles and miles of dusty mountains and empty highways, I see a diner on the side of the road. I pull over, hoping like hell there will be somewhere close by where I can get some sleep tonight.

Inside, there's a guy sitting at the table who introduces himself as Jonah.

I tell him I'm Cole Mills -- the alias I've been using the last four weeks. No one needs to know I'm Colton Miller. In fact, part of me wishes I could leave that entire life behind.

When I ask where I am, Jonah tells me I'm ten miles shy of the town of Eagle Crest.

He's wearing Carhartt's and a trucker hat, has shaggy hair, and a sleeve of tattoos on his arms. He offers me a genuine smile--something those hipsters in L.A. would never give a stranger.

"Never heard of the place," I say as a waitress comes over and refills Jonah's coffee.

"Well, there are about two thousand people in the town of Eagle Crest," he tells me, "but we've got families all over these mountains, lots of good folks around these parts."

"Can I get you something, sweetheart?" she asks. Her name tag reads Rosie.

"I'm good, thanks. Just looking for a hotel."

"Oh sure," Rosie says. "Laila and Virginia have a little hotel."

"Yeah, and it's the best bed and breakfast in the state," Jonah says.

Rosie rolls her eyes. "It's only a few miles away, in Eagle Crest."

Relief floods my face. "Thank God. I was thinking I might have to sleep in my car."

Jonah laughs. "Hell, we'd have found *some* place for you to stay."

"So, what town is this?" I ask.

Rosie smiles warmly. "We like to call it Miracle Mountain," she says.

I raise my eyebrows. "Lots of supernatural mysteries take place here?"

She and Jonah share a look. "You could say that," she says. "When people come here, they seem to stick around is all."

"Well, sorry to say, I'm just here for the night," I tell them. "I'm headed to Washington tomorrow, to the town of Linesworth. You ever heard of it?"

"A little tourist town, right?" Rosie says. "I've been begging my husband, Buck, to take me there for a weekend away."

"I've never been there myself," I tell them. "But I hear it's really pretty this time of year."

"I hear it's a cool place any time of year," Jonah says. "Lots of skiing there in the winter, and apparently, they have some world-famous cinnamon rolls."

Rosie slaps Jonah's shoulder playfully. "And what's wrong with my cinnamon rolls?"

Jonah laughs, then gives me the address of the hotel, and even draws me a little map when I tell him my phone doesn't get reception.

"Come back if you get lost, okay?" Rosie says. Jonah shakes my hand as if we're long lost buddies.

I thank them, then get back in my car, driving away as the sun sets, glad I grew out this beard. Back home, I couldn't leave the house without being recognized; without the fucking paparazzi on my ass. As I've been on my month-long road trip, traveling through Wyoming, Montana, and now Idaho, no one seems to give a fuck about what films I've starred in, they don't seem to care that I have an Oscar on my mantel. They look me in the eyes when we talk and assume the best.

It makes me wonder why in the hell I've spent so much time with people I don't really like all that much.

Following Jonah's directions, I drive a few

miles, make a few turns, and find myself in a low valley, right outside of the Eagle Crest Bed and Breakfast. There are only a few cars in the parking lot, but the house is beautiful.

It's an old farmhouse, a sweeping porch with rocking chairs out front, and even though it's getting dark out, the silhouette of the mountains surrounds us.

I grab my suitcase from my trunk, knowing how badly I could use a shower after driving in the heat all day. My stomach growls and I wonder why I didn't sit down at Rosie's Diner and order a slice of pie.

I pull open the door to the B&B and the quiet wraps around me.

"Hello?" I ask. But no one answers. I set down my suitcase, and call out another hello, but still nothing. Past the foyer, there is a sitting room, and opposite it, there's a dining room with half a dozen tables. Past the room, French doors are slightly open and I see someone sitting in an Adirondack chair, reading.

I move towards the doors, pausing before stepping out.

Sitting there, reading in the moonlight, is a woman who stops me in my tracks. She has soft brown hair and full pink lips. An upturned nose and thick black lashes and a petite body curled up in that chair. She's looking at the Kindle in her hands and completely wrapped up in whatever book is on the screen. I lick my lips, knowing what I want. Her.

"Hello?" I call again, this time, her chin lifts, her eyes find mine and a smile fills her heart-shaped face.

All day long, I've been lost on the road.

But one look at her and I know I've been found.

Chapter Two

LAILA

It's been a long day of cleaning rooms, washing sheets, and restocking toiletries. I do the beds and Virginia does the breakfasts. It's not exactly glamorous, but the job is ours; we're our own bosses, and it's a life I can take pride in.

It's something I didn't know I'd ever be lucky enough to find.

I wouldn't say I'm exactly happy, though; not yet. Most people I've gotten to know here always comment that I have a sad look in my eyes. I still have a long way to go to get to a place where I am genuinely at peace. Not surprise after everything I've been through. But Virginia and I have been here in Eagle Crest for a year now and I'm beginning to make a few friends, to trust the people I've gotten to know.

Virginia has already left the B&B for the night, though she didn't have to go far. We have a shared apartment over the detached garage, and so walking home from work only requires going twenty yards.

But I'm not ready for bed. Dusk is my favorite time of day. After our guests have retired for the evening, I like to come out here to the patio where I light the citronella candles to keep the mosquitoes at bay. I drape a blanket over my knees to keep me warm and sit with my Kindle to keep me company. It's a simple life, but it's on my terms -- no one else's.

I'm just settling in with a glass of white wine, engrossed in my book when a voice startles me. I look up, realizing I have company.

"Oh, hello," I say, setting down my Kindle on the side table next to my wine. "I didn't see you there."

"Sorry, I didn't mean to scare you," he says, walking onto the patio. He has a thick brown beard that causes a wave of desire to roll through me, but it's his eyes that really reel me in. They are the kind of clear blue that you could get lost in. That you could drown in.

He's tall, broad-shouldered, and his bicep muscles stretch out his T-shirt sleeves. His arms are free of tattoos, but he's tan as if he's been driving for miles on end with his arm out the unrolled window, the sun beating down on him.

"I'm not scared, are you looking for a room?" I ask.

He nods. "I am, do you have any available?"

"A few," I say with a smile. "Are you looking to stay a while or just one night?"

"Just one night."

"How did you hear about us?" I ask, standing up from my chair.

"I got lost and my cell reception is shot. Stopped at a little diner a while back and they told me to come here."

"You must have been at Rosie's."

"That's the one."

"And you didn't bring me any of her famous pie?" I tease.

"Man, I wish. I pulled up here thinking about that pie."

"Well, you'll have to get yourself a slice on your way out of town."

"Will do," he says, looking around the patio as if taking in every detail. "So, are you Virginia or Laila?"

"Gosh, sounds like Rosie was chatty tonight."

He laughs. "Well, a guy was there, too, Jonah, and he only had good things to say about this place."

I smile. "Oh, I'm sure he did. He has a thing for Virginia."

"So, you're Laila?" He looks me in the eye when he asks and as I nod, I feel my heart go thump-thump-thump. Which is something it hasn't done in a very long time.

Not since before the Badlands. And that seems like it was forever ago. A different lifetime.

But this man stirs something in me. Muscle memory maybe, the desire to be held and touched and wanted. To be something more than the broken girl who was used and abused.

I swallow, hard, biting past the emotions of my past, and he reaches out his hand to introduce himself. "I'm Cole Mills."

I nod. "Laila Adams."

"You work here long?"

I shake my head, thinking that Cole seems chatty. Maybe he's been lost and driving in circles for too many days. "Would you like to sit and have a glass of wine?" I ask, pointing to the open bottle.

He lifts his eyebrows. "You sure?"

I nod. "I'd love company. Just give me a sec." I step inside the French doors and head to the kitchen. Once there, I grab the lemon cake I made this afternoon, two forks, and a wine glass. Then I head back to the patio.

Cole takes the wine glass from my hand and eyes the two-layer lemon cake.

"Why would I want to go to Rosie's for pie when I can eat cake here?"

I smile. "Well, some people are pie people, some are cake people--"

He cuts in, "And some people are both."

Laughing, I offer him a fork, then pour him a glass of Riesling.

"I like you already, Cole," I say playfully, appreciating his warmth. I haven't felt this kind of attention from a man in a really long time. Maybe ever.

"You've lived here awhile?" he asks and I remember his question from a few minutes ago.

"Actually, Virginia and I just moved here and opened the hotel a year ago. We've been best friends for a long time and decided to go into business together. We'd been through a rough couple of years, but when we got an unexpected settlement, we took the money and opened the B&B. It was kind of our restart button."

"Wow, that's great," Cole says, listening intently as we both sit in Adirondack chairs. "So, now you're living in this place I hear is called Miracle Mountain?"

I laugh -- Jonah and Rosie really must have given him an earful. "Well, it isn't technically Miracle Mountain. The B&B is in Eagle Crest proper. The mountain range they are referring to is just north of the diner."

Cole nods. "They say when people come there, they never seem to leave."

I lift a forkful of cake to my mouth. "That's what I've heard. Lots of romance is in the air over there."

"But not here?" he asks, looking at me, and I know what he's getting at.

"Not here." Then I give him a wistful smile, pointing to my Kindle. "Though I love to read about other people's happily ever after."

"Not sure you believe that you'll find one yourself?"

"Not likely. But that's part of why I wanted the B&B, something I can call my own. So even if life beats me down, I know this place is waiting for me."

"You're quite a cynic for someone so young, and so damn beautiful..." He stops himself, probably realizing I've dropped my eyes to the ground; how my body almost curls in on itself. "What did I say?" he asks softly.

I shake my head. "It's nothing."

"Bullshit. What did I say?"

I shake my head again, waving a hand in the air. "It doesn't matter, Cole."

"Of course, it does."

"Truthfully?" He nods and so I continue.

"I've just been hurt by a lot of men who wanted me because of the way I looked. They saw me as an object, not as a person. And it kinda…" I let out a long breath, then bite the side of my lip and shrug. "It messed me up pretty badly."

Cole nods slowly as if understanding. "Right, so my leading with how pretty you are doesn't exactly bring warm, cozy memories to the surface, is that it?"

I nod, feeling the heat rise to my cheeks. "Sorry to put my baggage on you."

"Are you kidding me?" Cole snorts. "Laila, I never meet women like you."

I lift my eyes. "Like what?"

"You're honest; it's refreshing. We all have shit, right? But most people spend all their time trying to cover it up. Pretend it isn't there. Like it's a dirty secret instead of the truth."

"And what's the truth?" I ask, wanting to know how clearly this stranger actually sees me.

"The truth is our history isn't something to be ashamed of--it doesn't have to define us, but it sure as hell makes us who we are."

"And who are you?" I ask him, this mountain man who rolled up here tonight, dusty from a long day's drive, sun-kissed from the Idaho summer, with eyes that seem to see straight through me.

He leans in, and at that moment, the mountain air stills and it's like anything is possible.

"I think I'm a man hoping for a miracle of my own," he says with a voice that is so gentle, yet so masculine, so absolutely concrete, that I realize I feel safe with a man for the first time in my entire life.

"Then it looks like you came to the right place," I whisper, smiling despite my fears and my inhibitions and my baggage and my pain. I smile, not knowing what comes next, but hoping that for tonight I can swim in his eyes and drown in his arms.

Then he leans over. And he kisses me.

It's a kiss that feels like coming home.

Chapter Three

COLTON

She just told me there have been a lot of men who didn't respect her, and then here I am kissing her. Her lips are soft like rose petals and her hair smells like purple lilacs in the summer sun, and I could do this all night. But I don't want to kiss her if she doesn't want to kiss me.

I pull back. "I'm sorry," I tell her. "I should have asked."

Her dark eyes grow darker and her thick hair swishes in gentle waves as she shakes her head. "Don't stop," she says, her voice catching.

"Are you sure? I don't want--"

"I'm sure," she says, cutting me off. "I like this, being here, with you. It feels right. I feel... safe with you."

I clench my jaw, amazed at her vulnerability,

the honesty that falls from her lips. No hidden agenda, no desperate clawing for my money, my fame, my notoriety. No. She just likes being here with me.

Have I ever had a woman say such a thing to me? Care whether or not I could protect her, whether or not I could watch over her? Be her rock, a goddamn knight in shining armor? I push my fingers through Laila's thick dark hair, the wine and cake forgotten, the sky dark, the night ours.

"Kiss me," she murmurs and so I do. I kiss her, pulling her into my lap, holding her there like she is right where she belongs. With me. A stranger.

My palm cups her cheek, as her pink lips part, as I find her tongue and kiss her with abandon. Kiss her like we both need to be kissed. Kiss her like this is where we both should be.

I run a hand over her back, wanting to touch her, to feel her. I want her bare skin under my hand, I want to explore each inch of her body. I want it all. Her.

"Oh, Cole," she moans between kisses, and my cock grows hard with her sitting in my lap, her ass against my length.

"God, I want you, Laila," I confess, my breath hot against her ear as I kiss her, inhale her. Make plans to devour her.

"Take me to bed," she whispers.

I nod, standing, and she takes my hand in her hers, leading me through the house, plucking a key from behind the front desk. I grab my suitcase, and she leads me down a hallway to the last door on the left. I watch as she slides the key in the lock, turns the knob.

As she unlocks the door I take in her slender hand, then her curvy hips, her round ass. Her long hair, the wavy locks tumbling down her back. She looks over her shoulder at me, and we share a smile that can only mean one thing: now.

In the room, I drop the suitcase and she locks the door. The light of the moon filters through the sheer curtains and for a moment we stand still, staring at one another. Her eyes rake over me and I memorize her and I want it all.

But mostly, I want that miracle this place promised.

I want this night to never end, for her body to be on mine, for my hands to run over her skin and show her that not every man is a sack of shit. That not every man is looking for a piece of ass when they look at her.

Because yes, she gets me hard, but when I stand here, looking at her, I see something else. Something more.

"What is it?" she asks.

I step toward her, my hands on her cheeks, my thumb running over her lips, cupping her cheeks, retracing her story. "When I look at you, I see a woman who is a fighter, who is strong. A woman whose story I only know a sliver of, but can already see that she is more than the sum of her past. She came here, to this valley, and carved her own destiny. That is courage, and that is fucking beautiful."

Tears well up in Laila's eyes, and when they fall, I brush them away. I hadn't expected her emotion, but I fucking feel what she feels. Everything.

"Why are you being so nice to me?" she asks.

"I'm not always like this," I tell her honestly.

"I don't believe you. What you just said, those aren't canned lines." She blinks away the tears and licks her lips and her pink tongue is so cute and sweet and l want her. Bad.

"What do you believe?" I ask her.

"That everything happens for a reason," she says softly, then she reaches up inside my soul and fucking sees me as the man I could be. Hers. Here.

Miracles.

I pull her to me, her lips on mine once more, and this time it isn't a kiss, it's a deep breath, it's a long sigh, it's the beginning of something real.

I run my hands over her shoulders, kissing her deeply as she unbuckles my belt. We peel off shirts and pants and shoes. I unhook her lacy bra, she pushes down my boxers, I watch as she steps out of her panties. Within seconds, we're left standing in nothing and we're ready, both of us. To be undone.

We collide, our bodies needy and wanting. Her skin so soft and smooth, and I run my hands over her, cupping her round ass, my fingertips tracing her hard nipples. Her breasts are full and big, and I want to push them together, around my cock, I want to kiss her areola, lick her nipples and run my hand between her thighs, feeling her warmth, her need.

She whimpers as I kiss her, and her hand finds my growing cock, the thick ridges against her soft hands, and damn, I'm fucking scared I'll lose it too damn fast. She overwhelms me in the best fucking way. She's not sugary sweet, she's a woman with depth and desire and no frills, no fuss. She's sad and she's alone and I want to make her happy. We can start with right now, with tonight.

I lay her on the bed, and I lie beside her, wanting to look into her eyes and I explore her exquisite body.

"Your body is so warm," I tell her, careful to

choose words that are sincere, that push me to look beyond her beauty and see her core. "I want to touch you, all of you."

"Please do," she asks, leading my hand to her pussy. She rolls onto her back and I lean down, kissing her nipple, swirling my tongue over her hardened bud. Her knees drop as I run my hand over her mound, my fingers running up and down her creamy slit. Her cunt is ripe and ready, and when I slip a finger inside her, she's so wet that I groan in pleasure.

"God, your pussy is tight," I tell her. "It feels so fucking good, Laila."

She closes her eyes as I touch her softly, my fingers fluttering over her folds, and even though I'm dying to move against her harder with my hand, to make her pussy pour with pleasure, I take my time, wanting her to open up on her own when she's ready.

"More," she asks, and I oblige, my only desire is to make her happy right now.

I move to the floor, kneeling before the edge of the bed, and I slide her down on the bed, so I'm right between her knees, then I dip my head and lick her creamy cunt. She moans as I flick my tongue over her swollen clit; it's so hard and needy and it makes me want to get her off all the more. This girl has been through hell and back and I want to make her feel like she's died and gone to heaven.

I press my mouth against her pussy, her sweet, juicy cunt so warm against my lips. My tongue runs up and down her, flicking her the way I know she needs. She's panting with desire, my beard tickling her pussy as I lick her. "You like that, baby?" I ask, and her moaning tells me that yes, she fucking loves it.

I kiss her thighs, my fingers moving to her ready cunt, and I press one inside her tight little hole, my cock raging as I do. God, my cock wants to bury itself inside her, but first I want her to scream my name, to come against my hand as an orgasm rocks her fucking world.

"Make me come," she moans, and it makes me smile, her lack of inhibition, her want. She has been through some shit, but her body is new to me, we are new to one another, and that means when I touch her, all of it's our firsts.

The first time I flick my finger over her clit, she clenches the sheets as she begins to feel the pleasure rolling over her.

The first time her knees buckle, as I dip a third finger into her creamy cunt and make her scream my name.

The first time she comes against my hand, her back arching, her words loud and so goddamn clear.

"I need your cock, Cole. My pussy needs your cock so badly."

I move to the bed, leaning over her. Her face so sweet but her words so filthy. It turns me on, make me so fucking ready.

"Where do you need my cock, baby?" I whisper, blowing in her ear. "Where do you need it?"

"Right here," she pants, guiding my pulsing length into her cunt. "Right here, Cole."

Chapter Four

LAILA

I've been with guys before. Ones I knew for years. Ones who hurt me and hit me and never looked into my eyes, who never cared about my heart. They wanted my body and they took what they wanted.

Cole is nothing like those guys. He is a man who doesn't take... he gives. When he leans over me on the bed, his eyes search mine as if looking for an answer only I can give.

I want to give it to him.

All of it. All of me.

"Oh, Laila," he groans as he eases his cock inside of me. I wrap my arms around his neck, needing to hold on to something. Needing to hold onto him. "Are you okay?" he asks again.

I nod. Never having been with a man like this before. One who is tender with me, holding me in his arms as if I am something precious. As if I am his.

Tonight, I am.

"I want this, Cole," I whisper, our noses touching, my eyelids fluttering, my chest tight. Is this what everyone feels like when they give themselves to a man who asks permission? Because right now I feel absolutely seen.

If it is, it's all I want. His cock is big and fills me up in a way that makes me gasp, and he cradles me in his arm, kissing my forehead.

"You're so tight, baby," he says, kissing my ear, sending hot air over my skin and making every inch of me tingle.

I moan in a response, but words are lost on me. My body gives into this moment and I rock in rhythm with Cole. His strong chest and broad shoulders cover me, enveloping me with a sense of security, and yes -- on paper, he is nothing more than a stranger, but in practice, he is holding my heart.

"Oh, god," he groans, thrusting against me as I wrap my legs around him, he rolls me over on the bed, so I am sitting on top of him. Looking down at him I'm caught off guard by how handsome he is, yet when he looks at me he somehow makes me feel like I am the most beautiful thing he has ever seen.

"God, you're perfection, Laila," he says as I

rock my hips, his hands cupping my full breasts. I lean down, and he pulls my tits in his mouth, sucking them, tasting me. And my pussy tightens as a wave of desire rushes up and over me.

"I'm so close," I whimper as his strong hands hold my hips. My long hair falls in my face, the ends grazing his chest and he tucks a loose strand behind my ear, pulling my mouth to his. His tongue explores my mouth and every touch makes my heart pound in my chest. I've never felt so alive, so lovely, nor so wanted.

Emotion floods me as an orgasm washes over me. "Ohh, Cole, yes. Oh , God, yes," I cry, the sensations are so overwhelming. He holds me steady and I close my eyes, never wanting him to let me go.

"Girl, I'm gonna come in you," he tells me as if it's a warning. I take heed.

"Good, I need it," I tell him. "I need you to fill me up."

And I do because when he does, tears prick my eyes and I lose myself in the ecstasy. I fall on his chest as we come together, my skin slick with sweat and his body hot against me. He cups my ass, kissing the top of my head as I lie in his arms.

"What was that?" I ask when I finally catch my breath.

"I have no fucking clue," he says. I look up, propping my chin on top of my hands. "But it was the best sex of my life."

I laugh. And I'm not a laughing girl. I'm the sad one, the broken one. The mess and the mistakes.

In Cole's arms, I feel like more than that girl. I could be his girl.

That causes my breathing to shallow, and it's like an ice cold bucket of water is poured over me, waking me up and setting me straight.

Cole doesn't really know me. That is why this feels so good. If he really knew me, he wouldn't want what he now holds in his arms.

He should have a sweet girl full of sunshine and rainbows; a girl who believes she deserves a happily ever after. He has clear eyes and an easy smile; he is like a blanket of warmth, and the last thing he would want is to spend his life wrapping me up and keeping me tucked in, nice and tight.

"I should go," I whisper, already thinking about how late it is, how soon tomorrow morning will be here.

"Don't go," he says. "You can sleep here."

"I can't. I need to work tomorrow and..." My words trail off. How am I supposed to say the truth?

I'm scared of you waking up and seeing me as a

girl who grew up in a trailer park, who had sex for the first time when she was fourteen--with a boy who was really a man who should have never done what he did. A girl whose innocence was taken before she was ready. I'm scared you'll ask me questions and find out I was a whore for the Badlands motorcycle gang. Caught in a cycle where I couldn't get free. At least, not on my own.

I don't want Cole to know that. Right now he thinks I'm beautiful. I don't want him to see me as I really am.

"Thank you," I whisper in the dark room, rolling from him. Inhaling him one last time. He smells like a man who knows who he is. Strong and confident and so damn sure of himself. And what he is is good. So, so, good.

He reaches for my hand. "Stay."

"I'll see you in the morning," I say, trying to stay strong, wanting to keep the memory of the night for what it was. One night, nothing more. One unexpected, perfect night.

I don't need more than that. I'll be living on the memory of this night for years.

I pull on my clothes, feeling Cole's eyes on me and when I reach for the door he speaks. "Laila, you gave me a night I will never forget."

"Me either, Cole, me either."

Then I leave the B&B and walk to my apart-ment. Inside, I tiptoe to the bathroom, turn the shower on as high as it can go and step inside and replay the night in my mind as warm water tries to wash away the pain from the past. The pain I carry with me everywhere, every day. The heartache I can't seem to erase.

COLTON

I wake up, not knowing when I last slept so well. After Laila left, I thought I'd toss and turn all night, but when I rolled to my side, looking out the first-floor window, I saw her steal across the lawn to a cottage behind the farmhouse. Her hair trailed behind her as she ran, the moonlight shining down on her, illuminating her beauty, and she reminded me of the miracle I wanted to find.

She is the miracle.

I take a shower and pull on clean clothes, wishing I didn't have to drive over the mountains. But I'm due in Linesworth today and I can't skip out on work. I'm starring in the movie, for fuck's sake. I'm just glad Rick and Rozzy didn't find me over the last month. Going off the grid was a smart fucking move.

Leaving the room, I roll my suitcase into the lobby with one goal in mind: Seeing Laila before I go and figuring out when I can see her again.

Someone is singing an old Jackson 5 song down the hallway, and the voice carries toward me. "Morning," the woman who was singing says, passing me and heading into the dining room. "Were you the late-night check-in?"

"Yeah, Laila helped me. Is she around this morning?"

The woman twists her lips. She's traditionally beautiful: blonde hair, tall. The kind of woman I usually see on the movie sets. "She's in the laundry room. She should be out soon." Then she cocks her head. "Do I know you from somewhere?"

I shake my head. The last thing I want to do is draw attention to myself right now. "Don't think so. I live in Los Angeles. Have you ever lived there?"

The woman laughs. "Um, no. I'm from Wyoming originally."

"Nice state. Just drove through there."

"Nice?" The woman lifts her eyebrows. "Not sure about that. I only have bad memories of the place. I'm Ginny, by the way. Well, Virginia."

"Nice to meet you."

"Are you hungry?" she asks.

"Starved."

We enter the dining room and the scent of eggs and bacon fill the air. Hot coffee is in a percolator and fresh from the oven biscuits sit in a heaping basket.

"Wow," I say. "This is quite the spread."

"Thanks," Virginia says. "Help yourself."

I take a plate and head down the buffet, keeping my head down as I find a table, not wanting attention from other guests. I'm dreading getting to Linesworth and being back in the spotlight. Out here in the country, no one seems to care or give any mind to who I am or where I'm from.

I look out the window as I eat, taking in the rolling hills and the mountain scaling behind them. The sun is out and birds are chirping, and I even see a deer jumping through the field. This place is more than a miracle. Hell, it feels like magic.

After I finish up, I push away from the table, disappointed that I haven't seen Laila. But as I walk back into the lobby, I see her behind the front desk.

My face breaks out in a smile as I take her in. She's wearing loose-fitting overalls with a white tank top. Her hair is piled on top of her head in a red bandana and she has on a pair of white Converse low tops. It's adorable and refreshing and so down to earth.

"Hey," I say, our eyes meeting as I step up to the desk.

"Oh, hey, Cole," she says softly, looking away.

Frowning, I reach over the desk, setting my hand on top of hers. "You okay?"

"I'm fine, just have a long to-do list to get through today."

"Sure that's it?"

She nods, licking her lips. "What else would it be?"

I run a hand over my beard. "I don't know. I woke up in a pretty good mood. I was hoping you did too. In fact, I was hoping I could see you again."

She exhales then bites her bottom lip. When she lifts her chin and looks me in the eyes again I see a depth in her that scares me. One that could swallow me up whole. Maybe last night I was so caught up in miracles and magic I missed it, but I see it now. Laila is more than I thought. Damn, this woman is everything.

"Look, Cole, I had a great time. But I'm not in a place for..."

"For what?"

"For you."

I clench my jaw. I can't remember, for the life of me, a woman ever turning me away. "Why?"

She sighs. "Because I'm just--"

"Scared?"

"Why should I be scared?" she asks, and her eyes go dark as if I'm tiptoeing too close to a truth she doesn't want me to see.

I reach over the counter and tuck a loose strand of hair behind her ear. "You said you've been hurt before, is all."

She pulls in a sharp breath and I know I am touching on something fragile. Her heart. "I'm not interested, Cole. That's it."

"Is there someone else?"

She scoffs. "No. Not even remotely."

"Than why?"

"Because I don't want to."

Shaking my head, I rap my knuckles on the desk. "Understood." I reach for my wallet to pay for the room, but she raises a hand.

"No, it's on the house, Cole. Please, just go."

I feel like I can read people pretty fucking well, and everything she is saying doesn't match with what I feel when I look in her eyes. "You sure this is what you want?"

Tears seem to brim in her eyes and she turns away. "I'm sure."

She's told me to leave more than once, told me men haven't seen her as a person. That she's spent her life being objectified, and the last fucking thing I want to do is add fuel to that fire. She asked me to leave, and as much as it kills me, I need to listen.

This is her life as much as it is mine.

I leave the B&B, get in my car and head down the long, empty highway. But I keep looking in my rearview mirror as I drive, and when I pass Rosie's diner, I know it's not pie I am craving. It's Laila.

Linesworth is a gorgeous place to shoot a movie about a man who got lost in the woods and eventually lost his life on the mountain. But even just a few days in, I can't help but wish I were somewhere else.

Most of the cast and crew are staying in a hotel on the edge of town and on my first morning off, I take a long walk into town, looking for coffee, and the scent of cinnamon rolls leads me to the Three Sisters Bakery. I remember Jonah and Rosie mentioning them the night I met Laila, and the memory brings a smile to my face. God, I wish I hadn't walked away from her. Laila made me feel content for the first time in a long-ass while.

The establishment is the quintessential tourist town destination, complete with display cases of dozens of fresh pastries and treats.

"Can I help you?" a woman behind the counter asks. Her name tag reads Maggie and I ask her what's best. "Well, my sister, Greta, makes amazing cinnamon buns. Can't come to Linesworth without having one."

"Sounds good. I'll take one, and a cup of coffee."

She smiles and serves me up. "You know, everyone is talking about the famous movie star, Colton Miller, being in town. It's an honor having you come to our bakery. My sisters are going to be jealous they missed you."

"If this cinnamon bun tastes as good as it smells, I'll be back," I say warmly. I grab a table in the corner and a few guys are sitting at a table next to me.

One of them raises his cup of coffee and gives me a nod like we're old friends. What is it with these towns in the Pacific Northwest? Everyone is so damn friendly, they might just give the South a run for its money when it comes to charm.

"You the actor here shooting the movie?" one of the guys asks.

I take a deep breath, assuming they're gonna want a selfie with me, or my autograph. Instead, they introduce themselves.

"I'm Charlie," one of them says. "My wife is the woman who rang you up, Maggie."

"And I'm Ansel."

"Ansel?" I frown, the name registering. "You live here, right?"

He nods, and Charlie cuts in. "Ansel is the author who wrote the book the movie is based on. Well, loosely based on."

"I thought so," I say, putting the pieces together. "Damn, it's an honor to meet you. I know the story of Luke is important to your family."

"Yeah, thanks," Ansel says, lifting his eyebrows and looking around the bakery. "Luke was Maggie's, and my wife Greta's, brother. So, it's close to home. Of course, the screenplay isn't exactly the story."

"Right, but still. I'm so honored to meet you."

"So, you like it here?" Ansel asks, taking the conversation off himself. He's the kind of guy I like. One who doesn't need to make everything revolve around him. Salt of the goddamn earth. Real men.

"Yeah, but..."

"But what?" Charlie asks.

"There is this woman. I met her on my way to town and I can't get her off my mind."

Ansel gives me an easy smile. "Classic story."

"Oh, yeah?" I give a small laugh. "I guess you should know, you're the writer."

"So, what is it about this woman makes her special?" Charlie asks.

I take a forkful of the cinnamon bun, thinking over how to answer. Sitting back in the chair, I try to find the words. These guys are practically strangers, but already I feel a real kinship with them. Maybe it's because I'm playing the part of their family member in this movie. It makes me feel like I can open up.

"Everything. Her eyes. Her smile. Her voice. It's like I would look at her and see a piece of myself I didn't know I was missing. The truth is, I only spent one night with her. Seems crazy to be unable to get her off my mind."

Ansel lifts his eyebrows. "Nah, not crazy. When you know, you know. Do you know?"

"I know I can't stop thinking about her." I run a hand through my hair. "Hell, sorry. I'm sitting here with strangers telling them my shit. Sorry. It's just, hell, it's been a long few months."

"Don't apologize," Charlie says. "I bet it's hard as fuck to find people to talk to when you're, well, you."

"You guys are strange, you know that? How is it that I can sit here, with guys I never met before and feel more comfortable than I ever have with the people back home in L.A.?"

Ansel shrugs. "Sometimes you have to leave the place you live to find your way home."

"Who said anything about home?" I ask.

Ansel claps me on the back. "You did, brother, the moment you said she was everything."

"So, I should try again?"

Charlie laughs, giving his wife a sappy glance. "You know the answer to that."

He's right. I do.

Chapter Six

LAILA

I'm grabbing the Tupperware container of corn and bean salad from the fridge when Virginia comes into the kitchen. Her eyes are wide and she's biting back a smile.

"What is it?" I ask, closing the fridge.

"He's here."

"Who?"

"Cole," She squeals, her blonde curls falling over her shoulder.

"Wait, what?"

"He's at the B&B. Came here asking for you."

"What did you say?"

She laughs. "I said I'd come to get you."

"Why?"

"Why? Um, because you've been thinking

about him constantly since he left a week ago. I've never seen you so sad."

I lift an eyebrow, knowing good and well what I've been saying. She isn't wrong, exactly.

"You deserve to smile, Laila."

"You don't get it."

Ginny snorts. "I'm the one who gets it the most. I know what happened at Badlands because I lived it with you. But that's the past, Laila. It's time you let yourself be happy again. Isn't that why we got this B&B, to give ourselves a chance to create our own destiny?"

I shake my head, wishing I'd never told her I slept with Cole last week. But Ginny has been my best friend for years. I owe my life to her and her brother, Bear. She had already figured out what happened before I offered her the details.

"I don't want to put my baggage on anyone else," I confess.

"I don't think he's asking for that. I think he was just wanting to take you on a date."

I sigh. "That's the problem, Ginny. I've never done normal things like that. Had a nice man ask me out and treat me well."

"Then it's time you started."

"And what if--"

She cuts me off. "Laila, not every man is like the men we knew. Look at Bear and Grace; he was a mess who needed her *grace* to forgive himself for the things he'd done. Maybe Cole is your Grace."

"This metaphor is getting weird."

"No, you're the one getting weird. Just go have fun, Laila."

I let my head fall back, knowing it isn't as easy as that. One night with Cole and I knew that nothing with him would be light and breezy. When we were together, it was intense. It was real. "I don't know. I'm headed to Cherish and James' place."

"Perfect," Ginny says. "Take Cole with you. Let him see the real you with your friends before you write him off. Heck, maybe one night on Miracle Mountain and he will be running for the hills."

Smiling in spite of the conversation, I grab the salad and head for the door. "You sure you don't need another set of hands at the B&B tonight?"

"It's your night off, Laila and you need it."

When I walk around the farmhouse, Cole is sitting on the porch swing, his eyes closed, sunshine streaming through the leaves in the trees and filtering across his face.

I'm caught off guard by just how handsome he is. His beard causes a tingle to run up and down my spine, and he is wearing a tee shirt that is tight around his biceps, reminding me just how strong and capable his body is.

"Hey," I say, sitting down next to him on the swing. "Fancy seeing you here."

He opens his eyes, and he exhales as if he has been holding his breath for an entire week.

"Laila," he says breathlessly.

"I thought I told you I wasn't interested?"

"I know," he groans softly, looking over at me like we've known one another our entire lives and not for just one solitary day. "But I had to try one more time."

"Were you driving back through town?"

He shakes his head. "No, I had the weekend off, so I thought I'd drive over."

"Where do you work?"

"All over. My home base is in L.A., but I'm doing some work in Linesworth, Washington, for the next month or so."

"What kind of work?"

"Boring stuff. Lots of talking people up and making people happy. Contracts and saying the right thing to the right people."

I lean my head back, lifting my feet off the ground and forcing the swing to move. "What would you rather do?"

He looks over at, smiling. "Sitting on this porch swing is pretty nice."

"Yeah, if only you could get paid to do whatever you wanted."

"You like running this place, though, don't you?"

I nod. "Sure, but I wish the profit margin was a little larger so we could hire a few people. Virginia and I are the only ones here."

"If you had more time off, what would you do?"

I smile, my eyes on Cole's. "Sitting on this swing with you is pretty nice."

"So, you're glad I came back?"

I sigh. "One day at a time, Cole."

"Damn, you are good at playing hard to get."

"This isn't a game."

He takes my hand and laces his fingers through mine. "I know."

"So, are you going to take me on a date, or what?"

"Of course I am."

"Good, because I already have plans."

"And what are those?"

"First, how are you with babies?"

When we get to Cherish and James' home, I notice that Cole is getting nervous.

"You okay?" I ask.

"Yeah, just, uh, I think I should tell you something before we--" But before he can finish, the front door is pulled open and Cherish is waving at us, telling us to come inside, that food is ready, and I ask Cole if it can wait.

"Of course," he says. "Just, uh, we don't know one another that well, and--"

"Cold feet about meeting my friends?" I laugh as I push open my door and grab the salad from the back seat. "Don't worry. James and Cherish are the nicest people in the world."

He nods, getting out of the car as James comes around the house, the mix of three and four-year-old triplets running around the porch and creating chaos that only happens when you have six kids under five.

"I didn't know you were bringing company," Cherish says as we walk inside her huge log home. She leans in and whispers, "I invited Jonah."

I pull back, scowling, watching as Cole and James trail behind us.

"Why did you do that?" I seethe. "I thought he has a thing for Ginny anyway?"

"Apparently, he's been shot down one too many times by her."

I snort. "What, so now you sic him on me?"

"Sorry." Cherish grimaces as she picks up one of her sons and sets him on her hip. "But who is this guy?"

"A guest at the inn. He came last week and then... I guess he wanted to see me again so he came back today."

"He's very attractive."

I smack her on the arm. "Cherish!"

"What? He is. I never knew your type. Honestly, didn't think this was it."

"What's that supposed to mean?"

"I don't know. He seems so..."

"Handsome?"

Cherish laughs. "Exactly. He looks polished, even with that beard."

"I honestly don't know much about him."

"Want me to grill him?" she asks, just as the men come into the kitchen. Jonah is with them. I feel bad for him; he always seems to be the odd man out.

"No," I whisper. "I want it to be..."

"Normal?"

I nod. "As normal as dinner with six kids, a man I've just met, and Jonah can be."

Chapter Seven

COLTON

Driving over the mountains early today, I'd been nervous. But sitting here now, I'm sure glad I listened to my gut and came back. Especially as Laila was clearly getting set up with this Jonah guy. He's nice, but he is all wrong for her. Jonah tells loud jokes, makes the table laugh, the toddlers crack up. He is all easy and nonchalant confidence.

That isn't the kind of man Laila needs. She needs strong and steady. She needs a man who can provide for her, take care of her, and give her what she has been dreaming of. A chance to sit back on the porch swing and take it easy.

I don't know everything, but I know enough to read between the lines. Laila has been through a rough patch that has lasted for most of her life.

"So, what about you?" James asks me. "What brought you to the B&B in the first place?"

I'm relieved no one seems to recognize me. In fact, they seem oblivious to the outside world, in a good way. They are too busy living their lives to know about Hollywood gossip and I can't imagine them getting a babysitter so they could go to the movies. Are there even theaters this far out in the sticks?

"I was all turned around. Stopped at Rosie's Diner and she gave me directions. Seems crazy that I got lost and ended up at Laila's doorstep."

"That's pretty romantic," Cherish says, passing around the platter of roasted chicken.

"How did you and James meet?" I ask her.

They share a smile and I look over at Laila, who has a soft smile on her face too. It's clear that these two women are close. And in a different way than Laila and Ginny are. From what Laila explained on the way over, she and Ginny are more like sisters-- but Cherish and Laila seem to share a connection I don't exactly understand yet. I want to, though. I want to know everything about her.

"We grew up together," James says.

"Where?" I ask.

"Not too far from here," Cherish says. She looks around the table, almost as if making sure her sharing is okay with everyone else present.

You can feel the way they respect one another. "But uh, we were, uh, well, we were in a cult."

"Shit," I say, leaning in and listening as they explain the circumstances that brought them together, apart, and back again. It's incredible, hearing how they fought for their love, for one another. How they knew in their hearts that their love was worth taking risks, going all in.

"And so then, after he took a bullet in the chest for me, I was free," Cherish says. "Jonah helped James every step of the way. We are all so lucky to have gotten through it at all."

I swallow, trying to find words for their love story.

"What about you, Cole?" James asks, wrapping an arm around his wife's shoulder and kissing her on the cheek. You can feel the love emitting from them both. "Have you ever been in love?"

"Not that kind of love," I say. "I've spent a long time caught up in the bullshit that comes with my job, with the city. That's why being here is such a breath of fresh air."

Jonah nods, adding some green beans to the tray on the highchair next to him. "That's the story most people have about coming to this mountain. It's like, when you come here, you get a second chance. You can start over."

"Is that what happened to you?" I ask him.

He shrugs. "Yeah, I mean, I lived in Florida with James for a few years, and dated women who were the opposite of the women here."

I lift my eyebrows. "Isn't that kinda a sweeping generalization?"

"Maybe," he jokes. Then leaning away from the toddlers, he says, "But I swear, there is something in the water here. That's why I won't sleep with anyone on this mountain unless I'm sure I want to have children with them."

"Oh yeah?" I ask, eyebrows raised.

"Yeah," he laughs. Then nodding toward Laila. "Be careful with that one. She has been through hell. She deserves the world."

I swallow, wondering if there is something between these two, but Laila just smiles warmly at Jonah, not a hint of red to her cheeks.

"Thanks, Jonah," she says. "You're so good at looking out for everyone. Maybe one day you'll meet a sweetheart of your own and can settle down."

James laughs. "Not if he keeps coming and going like he's doing."

"Hey," he says with a grin. "I like going to Spokane. Can't help it."

"It's not Spokane you like," Laila laughs, wiping a baby's face with a wet washcloth since dinner is over. "It's Tinder."

The table erupts with laughter, everyone

discussing Jonah's terrible taste in women, how he always seems to date people who realize that he's too good of a guy to say no.

I sit back, enjoying the conversation, how everyone pitches in, takes a baby in their laps, another round of beers grabbed from the fridge. When Cherish sets a little one in my lap I look up at her in surprise.

"What, not used to babies?"

"Uh, not exactly," I say honestly as I awkwardly hold the baby in my arms. "I'm an only child. Never thought about having kids myself."

Jonah laughs. "Then you better get off this mountain, stat."

Later, as we park back at the B&B, Laila grabs a blanket from the porch. "Let's got out to the field," she says, taking my hand. As we walk, she points out the studio apartment behind the farmhouse and the large lake being it.

"That's where I want to live someday. On the lake."

"Looks beautiful."

"You should see it in the daytime. Especially in the summer. Every time I look at it, I feel lighter. Which is saying something for me."

"Usually you feel heavy?" I ask.

"Kind of. I guess I usually feel a weight around my shoulders. A weight I can't shake, no matter how hard I try."

"What do you think it's about?"

She sighs. "Do you ever feel like maybe you don't deserve good things?"

I stop walking, pulling her to face me. "Don't say that, Laila. You deserve the whole damn world."

She smiles wistfully, as if unable to believe me. God, I wish she saw herself the way I see her.

We walk to an empty field, the sky above filled with thousands of stars. We lie on our backs, and I wrap my arm under her. I've been waiting for this exact moment all week.

"What did you think of my friends?"

"I think you're lucky."

"Why's that?" she asks.

"James and Cherish are good people. They are real."

Laila laughs. "And your friends in L.A., they aren't real?"

"Honestly? No. Not this real."

Laila exhales. "I get it. I never knew people were this good, this honest and hardworking and kind before I moved here. Men who took care of their children and women who wanted to watch them take their first steps." She hesitates. "My childhood wasn't like that."

"What was it like?"

"You want to do this, Cole? Because we don't have to. We can kiss and fuck and let that be enough. You don't have to --"

I cut her off. "I want to know you, Laila."

"There isn't anything good to know."

"I don't want the highlight reel. Give me the non-filtered version."

She swallows. "I can't, Cole. I mean, I just..."

I stiffen. "It's fine. I know you hardly know me."

"I want to ... I'm sorry ..."

"Look, don't be sorry. I don't want to push you to open up. I get it, it's hard to be real."

"What about you? What was your childhood like?"

Cole presses his lips to my forehead. "My parents pushed me. Hard. To be the best. And I'm grateful, in some ways, because it made me the man I am today."

"But?"

"There's always a but, right?" I pull Laila closer and breathe in her lavender shampoo, running my hand over her bare shoulder. "But my parents died in a car crash when I was twenty. That was ten years ago, but sometimes it still feels like yesterday."

"I'm so sorry."

"They were good people, sacrificed so damn much to give me more than they had. And I know I was lucky to have their love for as long as I did."

"You don't have other family?"

I shake my head. "Not really. A distant aunt, some cousins. But not family like I saw tonight."

"You told Jonah you don't want a family?"

"I think losing my parents scared me. What if something happened to me and I had a child? Who would care for them, raise them?"

"I get that," Laila says. "My fear of having kids is not doing it right. That I'd screw them up. My mom was... she was awful. I never knew my dad, so what do I know about family?"

"You think Cherish and James are crazy?" I ask her, thinking of their six children.

"I think they are really lucky. They went through hell, and yet somehow..."

"Somehow they are some of the happiest people I've ever met," I finish.

"Exactly." She sighs, turning her face toward the sky. Her profile takes my breath away. Her nose is so cute, her lips so full, her cheekbones so beautiful. She is exquisite and she hasn't the slightest idea.

"Did you and Jonah ever..." I ask.

Laila shakes her head. "No. He's not my

type."

"No?" My inflection betrays my feigned nonchalance.

Laila laughs. "I promise, he's not."

"Why is that?"

"He's a good guy, but still likes to play."

"You don't like a guy who plays around?" I ask, rolling to my side, and pulling her to face me.

"No. I'm not that kind of girl. I feel things deeply. I don't take anything lightly. That's why I..."

"Why you wanted me to go?"

She nods. "And even now, Cole. I can't promise this will last longer than tonight."

It kills me. The idea that she isn't sure where she wants this to go. Because I know. I want to see how far we can take this. I have a feeling it could go all the way.

"Do we have to make decisions right now?" I ask.

She shakes her head. "I don't suppose we do." A tiny smile plays on her lips.

"Good, because I'm not ready to say goodbye."

"What are you ready for?" she asks.

I pull her closer, cupping her cheek with my hand, drawing her lips to mine. "You, Laila. I'm ready for you."

Chapter Eight

LAILA

When he kisses me, I feel like the beginning layers that I've kept wrapped so tightly around me since the day I was freed from the Badlands, are falling away. In Cole's arms, the heaviness that always surrounds me begins to lighten.

"I missed you, Laila," he tells me. "It's only been a week, but damn, I need this."

I run my hands over his chest, wanting it so badly too, knowing how my thoughts have been tied up in him for days and how his coming back here is exactly what I was hoping for.

Still.

It's terrifying--having the one thing you want within your grasp.

It might be easier to push it away.

But I can't now. Not yet. Now his lips are on

mine, his hands in my hair, my legs are wrapping around him. This is happening. And as his hands run under my skirt, between my thighs, all I can think is, *oh, thank God.*

"I missed you too, Cole," I moan as he touches me, as his fingers slide beneath my panties, feeling my heat, my need. "Ohh," I whimper as his fingers flutter against my folds.

"You are so wet, baby," he growls in my ear, his beard tickling my cheek. My back arches as he moves lower, as he pushes up my dress, slides off my panties, spreads my knees. "I need to taste you."

His mouth lowers to my warm cunt, and his tongue runs up and down my slit, his strong, big hands on my thighs, squeezing me like he loves to hold onto me.

I run my hands through his hair, and then unbutton my blouse, unhooking my bra at the center clasp so my breasts can fall out. I massage my nipples; they are so hard and needy, and as Cole licks my pussy I touch my breasts more.

"You taste so good, baby," he tells me as he runs his thumb over my needy clit, and I moan in pleasure, knowing that this is the one thing I needed. A man's gentle touch to open me up.

"I want to feel you," I tell him. "I need to touch you, Cole."

He looks up at me, a wry smile on his face. "Not yet." Then he presses his mouth back to my pussy, sucking on me like he can't help himself, and an orgasm builds at my core as he licks me, his beard tickling me as my pussy begins to drip with pleasure.

"Girl, you are squirting all over me." He loves it. He begins to lick me up and down with intensity, in a way that makes my skin tingle with pride. He loves the way I feel against him and it makes me melt on the blanket, makes me forget my worries and fears--my everything. At this moment I am just here, with him.

I come, the orgasm starting at my toes and reaching my core, tears fight to escape my eyes as he gets me off in a way that is deep and real and raw.

"Please, I need you in me, Cole," I beg, inching myself up to sit, and Cole stands, taking off his pants. We strip to nothing together, our bare skin exposed to the light of the moon, the stars overhead, and it's as if time has stopped. It's just him and me here now. The sweet summer air stirs around us and Cole wraps me in his arms, and at this moment, my beating heart is his.

He pulls me to the blanket, and I sit on his lap, wrapping my legs around him as his big, thick cock fills me up. Our foreheads press together as he enters me, and I gasp, his size glorious and making my pussy explode in pleasure.

"Oh, Cole, you feel so good in me," I pant as his capable hands hold me at the base of my neck, at the base of my spine, holding onto me in such a tender way that all I want right now is to make him happy. Make him come, make his cock explode so deep inside me that he never forgets the way my body feels against his.

I rock my hips, the moment overwhelming me, and our eyes meet--locking together. We both need this. Need more. And this is everything.

He rolls me on my back and I scream his name as he thrusts deep inside of me, breaking down the walls around my heart. My body shakes as we touch and feel and explore every inch of one another's bodies. I kiss his neck, breathe hot air in his ear, let him take me. All of me. He comes deep inside of me and I beg him for more. More. More.

He gives it to me. Flipping me over and squeezing my ass, wiping my cunt with the blanket then massaging my hole. "I'm gonna come in you, baby, all night long."

"Please, please take me."

He does, his thick, long cock is hard and ready as he uses my pussy juice to work my asshole and I rock on my hands and knees, needing him to fill me up in a way I've never wanted so badly before.

"You sure, baby?"

"Please," I beg, and he begins to enter me, opening me up so intimately that tears fill my eyes. He asks if I'm okay, and I know if I said I wasn't he would stop. When his hands hold my hips I feel like he wants me to feel as in control of this moment as he is.

His cock moves inside me, sending shock-waves of desire through my body. I'm moaning as he takes me, my mind forgets the pain of my past and right now, right here, all I can think about is how good it feels to be touched by a man like Cole.

I press a finger to my clit as Cole fucks me from behind, I massage my swollen bud as Cole runs his hands over my ass, planting kisses on my back. He runs a hand over my breasts, massaging my still hard nipples, causing me to get off so hard I cry out as the orgasm rushes through me.

"Oh, God, Cole. Oh, oh, yes," I moan. He finishes inside of me, both of us full and exhausted and spent and needing more.

So much more.

We fall on the blanket, panting for breath, my fingers wrapping around his still-pulsing cock, massaging his tight balls, and I want to stay here, in this moment, forever.

The sky is a blanket of stars, stretching farther than the eye can see, and I want to bask in the glory of this night. In the beauty of Cole's body against my own. The euphoria is written on my face, the bliss undeniable.

"I think I fucking love you, Laila," he says, the words an echo of the glittering stars above—they're changing the whole night sky. Cole could do that. Change everything for me. But I'm not ready to accept that kind of devotion. My hand stills and throat goes dry.

Love?

He rolls over, propped up on his elbows, looking down at me.

I don't want to meet his eyes. Can't meet them.

Love?

"I can't do this, Cole," I tell him, sitting up, reaching for my clothes.

"Don't, Laila, don't run."

But I shake my head. "I'm not running. This is my home. It's you who should go."

"But why? Why does it scare you?"

"Because I don't know you, Cole. And..." I blink back tears.

"And what?"

"And I promised myself I would never let a man hurt me again."

"So, you'll do that by not letting a man in?"

I nod, pulling my clothes on. "Exactly."

"But Laila, I mean it, I love you."

The pure joy that had been written on my heart only moments before is gone. "That's not possible, Cole."

"Why not?"

I move to go, knowing I need to. "Because you don't even know me."

As I go down the hall of the B&B, opening the door to the room Laila gives me, I want to pull her in my arms and ask her to stay. Here. With me.

"You're sure?" I ask, knowing my question isn't a weak one. It's a fucking brave one.

"I can't, Cole, I just... can't." She turns to leave. Her shoulders are shaking, and I can't understand why she would rather go when she could stay.

It isn't how I wanted this trip to go. Maybe I was a fucking fool to think she would see me without the fame and fortune, and want me just as I am.

But turns out it isn't enough for her. She wants more than I can offer and it fucking slays me. Part of me wishes I had told her exactly who I am, but I don't want her to choose me because of my money. I want her to choose me because when she looks into my eyes she sees everything she wants.

As I leave town the next morning --after a sleepless night in a room at the B&B-- I stop at Rosie's Diner. Maybe it's wrong to go there, to grasp at straws for a life that isn't mine. Laila told me to go and so I will. But damn, it isn't easy.

"What can I get you, sweetie?" Rosie asks showing me to a table and offering me a menu.

"Coffee and a slice of pie, please."

"What kind of pie?"

I think back to my first conversation with Laila --about being a pie or a cake person or being both.

"The best you got," I tell Rosie.

She brings me coffee and banana cream pie, a warm smile on her face. "You look worse for wear. Were you at the B&B last night?"

I smirk. "I'm guessing people talk on this mountain just as much as they talk anywhere else?"

Rosie smiles. "Well, Cherish was in here earlier this morning, she told me you had dinner with her and James last night."

I nod. "They're good people."

"Sure are. Cherish and Laila became friends

real quick after Laila moved here last year. I was so happy that they found one another, they both had been through a lot with men who didn't treat them well." Rosie waves her hands. "Sorry, it's not my place to say that."

"No, it's fine," I say. "You mean with Cherish being in the cult?"

Rosie nods. "And, you know, with Laila being in that motorcycle gang. I know a bit about it all myself. When I met Buck, my husband, I was running from the Russian mob."

My eyes widen. Cult. Mobs. Gangs. Before I can ask any more, a big family comes into the diner and Rosie turns to them, a wide smile on her face. "Hey, Harper, Jax. You brought your whole crew!" She turns to me. "Sorry, Cole, I'm gonna go help my other customers. Let me know if you need anything."

I nod, trying to process what she said. I finish my pie, wishing Laila could have let me in more, given us more of a chance. Wishing I had been someone she felt safe enough to confide in. God knows I would have been her rock if she'd let me.

When I leave the diner, I wave on my way out. Rosie calls after me, "Don't be a stranger."

I keep my head down, and get in my car, driving away from the first town that I've ever set foot in that felt like home.

Back in Linesworth, I pour myself into the movie. My heart and my goddamn soul. God knows Laila doesn't want it. Want me. She made that loud and fucking crystal clear. After getting to know Charlie and Ansel, and their brother-in-law Clive, I learn that the character I'm playing in the film, Luke, was a real stand-up guy. It makes me want to fucking nail this role because Luke's memory deserves that.

And since Laila told me to go; not once but twice, I decide the last thing a girl as wounded as her needs is a man forcing her into a relationship she doesn't want.

Damn, is that what love is? Giving up what you want for someone else?

If it is, I don't want love. Not real love. Not this.

Because it kills me.

It also fuels my scenes every day when I show up on set.

Griff, the director is floored, in fucking tears when I deliver the monologue that closes the movie.

"What got into you, man?" he asks after he shouts *'That's a wrap'* to the cast and crew.

"You thought it went well?" I ask, knowing in my heart that I put it all out there.

"It's gonna win us an Oscar."

"Don't jinx it," I say, laughing. But deep down, I think he might be right. You can't fake heartache like this."

He smirks, then claps me on the back. "You killed it, Colton."

The compliment, from him; it really means a lot. "Thanks, Griff. It's always an honor to work with you."

"So, what's next?" he asks me as we walk toward the trailers.

"I don't know. I want out of L.A., I know that much."

"You're crazy, Cole. To be thirty in L.A., with millions in the bank. You're living the dream. So, you want out of L.A.? What does that even look like? And for what?"

I clench my jaw, thinking of Laila. Always thinking of Laila.

"I don't know. I'm gonna go home and lie low, try to figure my shit out." I think about how I turned my phone on for the first time in weeks, and how Rozzy had left hundreds of messages. How they had grown in their level of urgency.

Eventually, I trashed the entire phone, preferring no connection to the outside than *that one*. The worst part is, I brought it on myself. I am the one who took her out in the first fucking place. She seemed so normal, but after the date, I realized pretty damn fast it was an act.

Griff brings me back to the present. "That two-month road trip didn't give you any clarity?"

"Clarity?" I run a hand through my hair. "I thought so. But... I don't know, Griff. Do you ever feel like two parts of your life are competing with one another?"

Griff pushes his lips forward. "What, you mean like wanting to be a good dad, and all that shit but also loving directing and unable to stop being a workaholic?

"Yeah," I say, nodding. "How do you deal with that?"

He shrugs. "I always let someone down."

I swallow. "That's not what I was hoping to hear, Griff."

"Hey, you're in the prime of life. You can choose any movie you want, live anywhere you want, be anything you want. You don't get to complain about having it too good. No one wants to hear that shit."

"So, you think I should just go all in with what I really, truly want?"

Griff snorts. "Not if it means you won't be signing contracts for my films."

I shake my head, not feeling any closer to what I want: the woman who told me to go.

Chapter Ten

LAILA

I stare at the two pink lines; at my life changing before my very eyes.

"Well," Virginia says from the other side of the door. "What does it say?"

Sitting on the closed lid of the toilet, I reach for the doorknob and let the door fall open.

Ginny steps toward me, falls to her knees, wraps her arms around me. "Oh, sweetie."

I wipe the tears falling down my cheeks. "I don't even know how to find him, that's the worst part."

"Maybe he will come back."

I scoff, wiping my nose. "Right, because after sending him away two times, he'll really want to come back for a third."

"He said he loved you, Laila. You never know."

But I do. That last night, he asked me to stay and I left, without looking back. I was clear, but oh so wrong.

"I just don't understand why he used a fake name," Ginny says.

"We're not sure it's not him," I say, holding out hope that my baby daddy is more than a liar.

"Cole isn't on Facebook, Twitter, LinkedIn-- anything. There isn't any Google search at all that brings up his face with his name," she says.

"I know," I say, defeated. "So, my baby will never know its father. Is that the point here?" I drop my head in my hands.

"Shhh, no, sweetie," Virginia says. "That wasn't my point."

"Than what was your point?" I stare at the pregnancy test. I'm going to be a mother.

How am I going to do this on my own?

"I can't do this," I say, thinking of my own childhood. My mom who was never there, being alone... running away. And then, it only got worse.

"You have me," Ginny says. "You have everyone on this mountain."

"But I want him," I say, hating that I am the reason he isn't here.

"I know, Laila, but it's going to be okay."

I try to steady my breathing. "I can't work and have a baby and..."

"One thing at a time," Ginny says.

"You know how much of a mess I've always been." I set the test on the bathroom counter, walking into our shared bedroom. "Where will a baby even live?"

"I don't know, but those are details we can work out."

I look at my friend, the woman who has been a sister to me. Who saved me from the Badlands, the girl I owe my life to, and I feel like there's suddenly a great divide.

"What do I do?" I ask, falling onto my bed. We are barely keeping the B&B open as it is. I'm going to have medical bills and won't be able to work. "It's an absolute mess, Virginia."

Ginny sighs, lying down next to me on my bed. "What do you want?"

"I want Cole. A man who doesn't exist."

"And what else?" We face one another on the bed and I try to think.

"I want this baby to be happy and healthy. I want this baby to know it is loved."

Virginia nods. "We've gotten through a lot of stuff, Laila. You're a fighter. And you can't quit now."

I nod, trying to stop the tears from falling. "Right. So, I go to the doctor's and figure it out. One step at a time."

Virginia nods. "And you won't be alone,

you'll have me every step of the way. And Cherish too."

"Why didn't I make him pay when he stayed here? I'd at least, have his credit card records so I could contact him," I ask, hating myself for that tiny detail.

Virginia smiles, and I remember all the nights we spent like this, wishing we could get away from the Badlands, making plans to leave that would never come true. Two scrappy girls dreaming of a better life.

"Will life always feel so hard?" I ask.

Virginia shakes her head. "No. It's gonna get better. I promise."

"How do you know?"

"Because we moved to the place where miracles happen."

"You believe in that?"

"I choose to."

"Will you come to me with the doctor's?" I ask, scared of being alone.

"Of course, Laila."

We stay like that for a long time, both of us avoiding the work that needs to be done at the B&B. Everything else can wait. Right now, my world has been rocked and I need the dirt to settle before I can stand on my two feet.

The day of the doctor's appointment, I admit to being nervous. I don't know what questions might be asked of me, and I don't want anyone to ask about the dad.

The truth is, I don't have an answer for that.

Virginia, Cherish, and I sit in the waiting room, and we try to distract ourselves by reading magazines.

"These organizing tips are so unrealistic," Cherish says, balking at an article.

"You should write articles," I tell her. "The real perspective from a mom of many."

"Harper is writing a book about being a mom to multiples right now," Cherish tells me.

"That's awesome," Virginia says. "Not that I plan on being a mom anytime soon, but good for her. First, she wrote romance novels, now this."

"See, a baby doesn't have to stop you from chasing your dreams," Cherish says.

"Right, all those dreams of mine."

"Hey." Virginia elbows me. "What about the B & B?"

"We both know that's your thing," I tell her. "You're the one who really wanted to open that."

"Do you not like running it with me?"

I shake my head, "That's not it. I like being busy. But, I don't know, I can't see myself doing it forever. I am sick of cleaning up after other people. It's all I did in the Badlands. I was basically a sex slave and glorified maid. I want to be more than that."

"Um, speaking of more than that... Laila isn't this Cole?" Cherish asks, holding an entertainment magazine cover out to us.

On the cover is Cole Mills.

Except the cover's headline reads *Colton Miller: Is he the father?!*

I'm not one to stay up to date on current events, but I can put two and two together.

"Holy crap," Virginia says, grabbing the magazine and staring at the image of the father of my child. "I knew he looked familiar."

"You know him?" I ask.

"Not well, but he was in that famous movie, the one that won those awards, *Hawk Line?*"

"I've heard of that," Cherish says slowly. "Wait, he didn't tell you he was an actor? Like an Oscar-winning actor?"

I shake my head, trying to remember what he'd said about his job. *Boring stuff. Lots of talking people up and making people happy. Contracts and saying the right thing to the right people.* Also known as an actor.

My heart is pounding in my chest. He lied to me. About everything.

Virginia is pulling open the magazine, scanning the article. She gasps and I bury my face in my hands.

"Do you want to know, Laila?"

"Just tell me."

"Some woman name Rozzy Thomas is stating that she is pregnant with his child, and he apparently refuses to take a paternity test, stating her claims are slanderous."

Cherish wraps an arm around me as tears fall down my cheeks. "It's okay, it's all going to be okay."

Is it, though? Cole kept everything from me and turns out he might be the father of another woman's child too.

Just then a nurse pushes open a door. "Laila Adams."

I reach for Virginia and Cherish's hands, clutching them to mine. "Don't make me go alone," I tell them.

"We'll be here every step of the way," Cherish says.

I hold on to them tight, thinking of how grateful I am. Because right now, they are all I have.

Chapter Eleven

COLTON

"**J**ust kill the story! Now!" I shout, pacing my house.

"It's not that simple," my publicist Mary says. "You have to take the test or this is just going to blow up. And then who is going to fix this mess? We need to try and get ahead of this. She already has the upper hand with the angle of this story."

"I won't give her that. It's exactly what she wants--"

Mary cuts me off. "It doesn't matter what she wants. It's what's best for your brand."

"Fuck my brand." I want to slam my fist in a wall. "Dammit, I spent a whole fucking month clearing my head of this shit, only to have it all thrown right back in my face the moment I get into town."

"Well, you could have told me this woman Rozzy and her brother were an issue. I can't help you when you refuse to tell me these things. And get yourself a phone, Colton. This isn't the dark ages."

"I don't want a phone. I don't want any of this."

Mary presses her fingers to her temples. "Any of what, exactly?" she asks me in a clipped tone.

"Any of the bullshit that comes with the job."

"What are you saying?"

"I'm saying the whole world isn't like this."

"Like what?"

"So damn concerned about lawsuits and bullshit magazine articles. I never even slept with the woman."

Mary lifts her hands, trying t get me to focus. "Then take the test and we can be done with this."

"No, I need to get out of town."

Mary groans. "Not again, Colton."

"Not again what?"

"You can't just ghost everyone for some Jack Kerouac bullshit."

"It's not bullshit. I need--" Just then Mary's phone rings.

Frowning, I look at Mary as she takes the call.

"It's who? No, I've never heard of that person. Just probably another crazy stalker. Can you handle it? Okay, thank you." She hangs up, turning to me. "No need to worry."

"Worry about what?"

"Apparently some woman is at our office downtown, demanding to get a meeting with you."

"Who is it?"

Mary waves her hand. "It doesn't matter. You need to focus on the Rozzy situation."

"It's not a situation. It's a--" Mary's phone rings again. When she takes it, I throw my hands up. "*This* is bullshit. I'm out of here."

She cups her hand over the phone. "Where are you going?"

"Far away." As I head toward my front door, Mary trails after me, but I'm not answering her questions. I hate the idea of this story being out in the world and I hate the idea of Laila getting her hands on it.

"Stop, Colton, how can I get a hold of you?" she hollers after me as I reach the foyer.

"You won't. It's called 'off the grid' for a reason."

She calls after me, clearly upset, so I pause and turn back for a moment. "I'm going to

Miracle Mountain, Mary. It's time I found my happily ever after."

"Miracle what? Happily who?" Mary shakes her head in confusion. "You need to tell me these things if you want me to do my job!"

"Then maybe I don't want you to do this job anymore."

"You don't want a publicist?" Mary scoffs as I pull open the front door.

"Maybe not, in fact, I don't really think I want this job at all."

"You don't mean that." Mary eyes me as if I'm crazy and maybe I am. Right now I feel insane that I ever left Laila.

"Here is what I do know, Mary, I don't want a life that is built on lies. I want a life that is real. And that doesn't exist in L.A."

I grab my wallet and keys and walk through the door. If I want Laila to take me seriously I have some things I need to clear the fuck up.

The private plane lands in Boise a few hours later. I may complain about my job, but it certainly has afforded me some perks. I spent the entire flight on the phone with a real estate agent named Louisa and I have plans to meet her tomorrow morning in Eagle Crest.

Now, though, I need to get to Laila. Explain a few things. Namely, tell her the truth about who I am. The last thing she needs is to have another man letting her down.

I rent a truck and drive toward the B&B. It's a two-hour drive, but with music blasting and the windows rolled down, it feels like no time at all. I listen to Bob Dylan singing about tangled hearts and all I can think about is that when I'm with Laila my heart isn't tangled at all. It is unfurled and whole and hers.

When I pull up at the farmhouse, I stretch my hands over my head and take a deep breath. It's do-or-die time right here.

In the foyer, Ginny is finishing a phone call. When she sees me, her eyes get wide. "Uh, gotta go," she says into the phone. She ends the call and walks around the front desk, mouth gaping. "What the hell are you doing here?"

"Looking for Laila. Is she here?"

"Is she here?" Virginia scowls. "What kind of question is that?"

"Uh, the most important one."

She scoffs, hands on her hips. "Interesting thing to say, *Colton Miller.*"

I exhale, knowing that is the worst-case scenario. Her finding out about me before I had a chance to set the record straight.

"Shit," I say, running hand over my full beard. "She knows then?"

"Yeah, and she's pissed. The last thing she needs is another man who is dishonest with her."

"I wasn't trying to--"

Virginia waves her hand in the air. "Save it for her."

"Right. I came here to tell her the truth. I'm trying to do the right thing."

"The right thing?" Virginia rolls her eyes.

"Why are you being so hard on me?" I ask her, genuinely confused. Yes, I didn't tell her best friend I'm an actor, but I'm here now, trying my best.

"Because Laila deserves more than a man who doesn't stick around."

And with that, Virginia leaves the foyer, and I'm left knowing I've fucked up the best thing that has ever happened to me.

Chapter Twelve

LAILA

No one returns my calls. No one gives me any information. And no one seems to care that I am in desperate need of reaching Colton Miller.

I realized he may be a player who has gotten some tabloid star pregnant, but that doesn't mean he hasn't also gotten me pregnant.

And he deserves to know.

Not that it matters since no one is taking me seriously in this town.

It's no wonder Colton spoke of L.A. with such disdain--I feel so far from the mountains down here. In the moment, I was sure coming alone was a good decision. I wanted to take a stand for myself and my child, I wanted to do this on my own.

Truth is, I had never even boarded a plane

before today. But Jonah drove me to the Boise airport and got me a ticket and asked me again if I was sure I wanted to do this on my own. Virginia thought it was crazy, chasing a man like this.

But that isn't what this is about. It is about giving Colton the chance to explain himself. Yes, he wasn't honest about everything, but when he looked into my eyes and told me he loved me... I think he meant it.

Which is why I want him to know about his baby. He deserves the truth. God knows no man ever offered me as much. But that doesn't mean I have to stoop to anyone else's level. I can be the best me and give him the benefit of the doubt.

After all, there are always two sides to every story.

Maybe this is just wishful thinking; holding on to hope that Colton isn't like everyone else. That just maybe he is the one for me.

Of course, the fact he also got some other girl pregnant complicates things slightly.

Finally, though, I am done being put on hold. Sitting in a coffee shop to avoid the sweltering heat of the city, I stalk the internet until I can find an address for Colton Miller. Of course, it may be a bogus address, but at least it is something to work with.

I get a taxi ride to the house in the Hollywood Hills, my eyes widening as I take in the gorgeous home. It is nothing like what you'd find in Idaho: it's modern, all glass and concrete and jagged edges and raw lines. I try to bury my embarrassment over what he must have thought when he stepped foot into the farmhouse. The B&B Virginia and I were so proud of. I remember telling Cole how proud I was to have something of my own. Was he laughing at me behind those gentle eyes?

I refuse to believe it.

But when I walk up to the gates of the house, I see someone else is already standing there, as if waiting to be let in.

"Who are you?" she asks in an accusatory tone. There is a car parked behind her with a man behind the wheel. I try to get a better look at him, but there is a bandanna covering his lower face.

"Uh, why?" I ask, not walking any closer.

"Because I'm Colton's girlfriend and so I should know the women coming around his place. It wouldn't be the first time that sack of shit's cheated on me."

I take her in. She is beautiful, with thick hair dyed dark red. Tall and slim and in a tight bodycon dress and wearing heels that tell me she means business. I look down at my

Converse and capris, feeling insecure. What was I thinking, showing up at a movie star's home dressed like I was going to fold some laundry?

"I didn't realize he had a girlfriend," I say, mustering up the truth.

"Well, he does." She purses her lips and I run a hand through my limp hair. I'm hungry and tired and confused. What exactly did I think would happen when I jumped on a plane?

"Okay, well, I just want to talk to him," I say. "So maybe we can go inside and--"

"You aren't going inside."

"Oh?" I step back, suddenly realizing something isn't right about this woman. Her eyes are wild and yellow around the edges. Her makeup is smeared and she keeps looking behind her at the driver in the car. He revs the engine.

"Why are you here anyway?" she asks me.

"I just... no reason. I just thought... you know what? It's all a misunderstanding," I say, hating that I've put myself in a compromising situation.

Then again, isn't that the story of my life?

"What did you misunderstand?" she asks, stepping closer. "What do you know? What aren't you telling me?"

Just then my phone rings. I reach for it in my purse but the woman is staring at me with an unhinged look in her eyes.

"I'm just gonna get that."

"Is it Colton?" she asks.

I frown. "Why would it be Colton? I thought he was your boyfriend."

"Put it on speaker," she says.

I begin to shake my head, but before I can do anything at all, I am pushed toward a row of thick hedges by the driver of the car. He has a gun pointed at my head and the woman has taken my phone. "You say anything about the gun and you're dead," she says in an even tone, as she presses 'accept' and puts it on speaker phone.

"Laila?" Virginia asks. "God, why didn't you pick up the first time?"

"I uh... uh..." I look at the man and woman holding me at gunpoint.

"What?" Virginia asks. "Sorry, it's hard to hear you. Anyways, I had to call because you'll never guess who just showed up at the Eagle Crest B&B?"

"Who?" I manage to eke out as the gun is jammed deeper into my spine. Tears begin to fall from my eyes and somehow Virginia picks up on my pain.

"Sweetie, you sure you're okay? Listen, I know why you can't reach Colton. He's here, in Idaho."

I gasp as the gun is pushed into my skin and

she mistakes it for amazement at what she is telling me.

"Anyways, he came to the farmhouse to see you. Of course, I was a bitch to him because I got all weird and protective of my bestie but, the thing is, I think he might have been genuine. And so maybe I was being too intense to him. Don't be mad."

"Not mad," I say. "Just--"

Before I can say any more the phone is yanked from my hand and shoved into the woman's purse.

"Come on, Rick," she says. "Looks like we're taking a little road trip to Idaho."

His hand is on my arm. "And what should we do with her, Rozzy?" he asks.

"Oh, she's coming with us. Collateral damage, if you will. Toss her in the trunk."

And with that, my past becomes my future.

I'm pushed into the trunk of the car, tears streaming down my cheeks. I fight back until the gleaming silver gun reminds me to stay quiet, and flashbacks from my teenage years crowd my mind. It was always like this. It's always been me being forced down, always being a pawn in a game I never wanted to play.

The rules were simpler when it was only me I was fighting for -- but now I am carrying Colton Miller's child. My baby.

They lock me in the trunk and turn on the car. As we roll down the highway, I don't kick or scream. No one will hear me on the highway.

But once I'm out of this trunk, all hell will break loose. I'll fight back. I'll fight for the girl I was and the girl I want to be. Fight for my baby's future, and fight for my own.

I just hope I get a chance.

Chapter Thirteen

COLTON

I call Louisa, the real estate agent, and explain a few things. Namely, I can't wait until tomorrow. I need to have that appointment now, today.

"I'm not sure I can rearrange my day, what was your name again?"

Since I first set foot on this mountain I've been lying low. But not anymore. Now I need to step up for Laila.

"It's Colton Miller. You may have heard of me." I grimace, hating how douchey I sound.

"Oh, uh, *the* Colton Miller?" she asks, her tone now ripe with interest.

"Yeah, the one and only."

"Well, I'm sorry, um, of course, I can see you. Where were you looking at properties again?" Louisa asks, flustered.

"On the lake in the valley outside of Eagle Crest."

"By the Bed and Breakfast?"

Yes, just past it."

"I'm not sure there is much out there…" I can hear her clicking on her keyboard.

"I know. But it doesn't matter. I'll buy all the land around the lake I can."

An hour later, I am parked on the side of the road, shaking hands with Louisa. She has just parked her wood-paneled Jeep Cherokee, which looks like it's been putting in miles in these parts for several decades. She's an older woman who looks like she was made from these mountains. Strong and confident, gray hair with clear blue eyes.

I immediately get the sense that I can trust her. A far cry from the acrylic nailed platinum blonde agents I've met in L.A., driving up in their sports cars.

"I must say, this is quite the surprise," she says with a chuckle. "I don't have time for games, no matter how rich or famous you are. Are you really wanting a place out here in the middle of nowhere?"

I smirk, appreciating her no-nonsense approach to me. "No games, ma'am. Just looking to put down some roots, to make a home. I was here a few months ago and fell in love with it."

She narrows her eyes as if making a decision about me. Finally, her face breaks out into a warm smile and she nods. "Well, you're a smart fellow, I can give you that much. No better place in the world than this mountain. Though Eagle Crest is getting a little big for its britches. Still, it's home for anyone with any sense."

"I couldn't agree more. Now, show me what this lake can offer."

"There isn't much like I said on the phone. But there is one little cabin tucked into one plot of land. It could be a good place to live while a bigger home was being built. That is unless you just plan on leaving it to a building company, and only coming here for vacation?"

"No, I plan on living here full-time. I leave for work a few weeks every few months, but I can fly in and out. If the property was big enough, I was thinking of getting my own landing strip."

Louisa's eyebrows raise. "A little fancy for this town, Colton."

"I know, but I need to make a living for my... for..." I want to say, wife. Lover. Partner. Soulmate. I want to say, Laila. But Laila isn't mine, not yet. So, I hold back. "I need to keep working. I love acting, but I don't want to live in L.A. This seems like the best option."

"I see that. Well, let me show you around then, city boy."

We spend the next hour touring the forty-acre property. There are acres of untouched, pristine land and I keep thinking of Laila and me, on that blanket, under the stars. Of her telling me how she wants to live out on the lake. I want to give that to her. I want to give her everything.

The cabin itself is tiny. One room with a moss-covered roof, but I know that would be a short-term fix. I want to design a dream house with Laila; give her everything her heart desires.

"I'll take it," I tell Louisa.

She grins, shaking her head. "You sure?"

"No question," I say, without a shadow of a doubt. "This is home."

After I've signed on the house, back at Louisa's office -- which is really just a trailer in her driveway -- I stop by Rosie's diner to purchase a peace offering for Laila. She wasn't at the B&B earlier today, but maybe she's back. I can bring her a pie and beg her to forgive me.

"Long time, no see," Rosie says as I step inside the comforting diner. There is a table full of burly mountain men in one corner, and Rosie is there, pouring them coffee.

As I walk toward her, I realize James is at the table, I haven't seen him since the night Laila and I were at his place for dinner.

"Hey there, Cole," he says, drawing a chair over to the table. "Take a seat, man."

"Been a while," I say, sitting down. James introduces his buddies to me, Jax, Buck, and Beau. Immediately I feel all eyes on me.

"Hey, aren't you, like, that actor?" Beau says.

James laughs. "Actor? This is Cole Mills, Laila's friend."

"No, I swear. I know it sounds weird, but when I was in the slammer we watched lots of action movies. You were in that one...what's it called, uh..."

"Number One Suspect?" I offer, knowing what role most guys remember me for.

"Yeah," he says, smacking the table with his palm. "I knew it. Nice beard, though."

James frowns, turning to me. "Dude, you've got some explaining to do."

Rosie pours me some coffee and I give the guys the rundown. My career, my road trip, my newfound lease on life in the form of Laila.

"So, I just signed on the dotted line, made an offer on the lakefront property. Gonna build a house out there."

Buck whistles low. "Shit, man, that's a nice plot of land."

Jax nods. "And Laila, she knows about all this? Because I know a thing or two about women. My wife, Harper? She likes to weigh in on the decisions. Maybe you should have asked Laila what she wanted before you decided for her."

"No, I know this property is what Laila wants. She told me. Hell, if she doesn't want me I'll build her the house of her dreams and stand in the wings for as long as it takes for her to give me a second chance."

At that, Jax gives me his nod of approval. "Good. If you love her like you say you do, you won't stop fighting for her."

All the men at the table grunt out their agreement, and I'm struck again by just how loyal and committed the men here are. I've never met people like this, and it fucking slays me to think about all that wasted time. Now that I've come to Miracle Mountain, I've learned a thing or two about relationships. Namely, they are worth their weight in gold.

"So, what now?" James asks.

"I came back to town to come clean. Turns out she already knows. She wasn't at the B&B, but Virginia told me. Said Laila won't want to talk with me."

Just then the diner doors swing open. In walks Jonah. Upon seeing me, he frowns. "What the fuck are you doing here?"

"What do you mean?" I ask.

"I mean, I dropped Laila off at the airport in Boise about ten hours ago. She was on her way to see you."

Chapter Fourteen

LAILA

I'm exhausted, thirsty, and so tired. When we pull up at a gas station in Winnemucca, Nevada, they let me out. It's the middle of the night and there is no one around. The man, Rick, presses the gun to my forehead and explains exactly what I'm to do when we go into the gas station.

I'm allowed to pee with Rozzy watching. I'm allowed to grab a bottle of water and a granola bar and set it at the register. I'm not allowed to speak.

So, I don't. Right now, all I want is to get out alive.

After we finish inside the mini-mart, I'm shoved into the back seat of the car. I give a silent prayer of thanks to the heavens for not being shoved back in the trunk.

I watch as Rozzy places a call to Colton. Hot tears well up in my eyes as her voice echoes through the car. I start to cry loudly, but Rick pulls out the gun and tells me to shut the fuck up.

I listen.

The call rings and rings and rings. Eventually, it's put on voicemail. "Hey Colton, it's me," Rozzy says in a syrupy sweet voice. "I miss you. And I want to see you. Call me. Please. I miss you. Oh, and I met a friend of yours, but I'm taking care of her. I hate to think you were cheating on me."

A moment later, her phone rings. A voice I wasn't expecting to hear slices through the dark car.

My heart pounds as I realize just how far I am from having the life I want.

"Rozzy," Colton says. "It's me."

"Colton?" Rozzy asks, her eyes wide with a thrill I can't explain beyond crazed. "Is it really you, baby?"

"Yes, it's me, baby. I don't know what you're doing, but I need you to listen to me--"

She cuts him off. "Did you see the article? We're having a baby!"

"I saw that, Roz." Colton's clear voice breaks my heart. "It's pretty incredible. You and me, having a family. I would have thought that it was impossible."

Rozzy beams and Rick gives a fist pump to the sky. As if everything they want is falling into place. Is Colton really having this lunatic's child?

"Listen, Rozzy, you said you met a friend of mine? What do you mean?"

"Some little slut was at your house. Said she was your friend, but I know better, Colton. I know you would never hurt me like that."

"Right, of course not. Was this friend Laila?"

Rozzy turns to me, glaring. "I don't know. She was a redneck white trash girl. Not what you need. She isn't me."

"Where are you, Roz? I miss you so bad," Colton says. "I need to see you."

"I know where you are, Colton," Rozzy says, her voice now thick with rage. "Don't lie to me. You are at that skank's house. Her friend said so this morning."

Rick turns around as I poorly stifle a cry. He presses the gun against my shoulder and I release a pent-up sob.

"Is that Laila?" Colton asks. "Do you have her with you now?"

"Why do you care?" Rozzy asks. "I thought you only cared about me?"

"I do, I do care about you. I just don't want anyone to get hurt."

"Well, I'll have to hurt her if you don't agree to my demands."

"What demand is that, Rozzy?" Colton asks, his voice shaking now.

"Sleep with me. For old times' sake. And claim my baby as your own."

"Anything you want, Roz. Just tell me where you are."

"No," she says. "I have to deal with this whore first. Then we can meet up. Just you and me. Together, forever."

"Rozzy," Colton cries. "Don't hang up, just stay on the phone a little longer. I want to hear your voice."

"Really?" she asks, her voice so sweet it could just about fool anyone. "I thought you forgot about me. You didn't return my calls. I thought..."

"I was just confused. But now I know. Now I know exactly what I want. Who I want. No more lies."

I weep as silently as I can, and Colton's voice whispers over the phone. "Don't cry," he says.

"That isn't me crying," Rozzy says glaring at me. "It's that skank. But don't worry. Rick is going to take care of her for me, and then we can run away together."

His breath is ragged and I can tell he is crying too. "Right. It will be just like that. You and me, starting a life together. I even bought us land on a lake, I'm gonna build us a house. Well, I found some men out here who will help. I'm not exactly a carpenter. But it will be just for you."

At that, I wipe the tears from my face. The barrel of the gun may still be pressed against my shoulder, but I am choosing to hear Colton's words as if they are just for me.

I bite my bottom lip. The lake. A house. A life together.

"I'm so sorry," he says. "I should have never left you. I know you've had a hard life and need someone you can count on. I know I should have fought for you."

Rozzy cries, tears of joy on her cheeks. "You remember me telling you all about that in the emails? How Rick and I spent all those years at that hospital? How my parents said we were crazy and couldn't be left alone? Well, I forgive you, Colton. I love you so much."

"I love you too." His voice cracks as he says it. "Just stay on the phone with me, Rozzy, I want to be with you forever. I don't want us to be apart for a single second."

I sit as still as a statue, knowing I am in a car with dangerous people; people who are unhinged--who might pull the trigger at any moment.

But then I hear the sound of a helicopter overhead.

Rozzy looks at Rick. Rick looks at me, finger on the trigger.

I look at the phone. "Colton, I love you too," I scream, knowing it might be too late.

My heart is racing as the helicopter prepares to land, Rozzy and Rick's vehicle now in clear sight. Rozzy made a fatal mistake in calling me. We could track her the moment the call went through.

And I wasn't wasting any time. I had a search team in place the moment the men and I put two and two together after Jonah showed up at the diner.

I need to get out of the chopper -- now!

I need Laila in my arms. I need to get down on one knee. I need her to know I will never, ever leave her side again.

"Go faster," I shout, the call now ended. The moment Laila shouted that she loved me, the line went dead.

Now, we land, and I am shoving my way out of the chopper, toward the car. As I make my way through empty the parking lot, toward the car, Rozzy and Rick push out of the vehicle, dragging Laila behind them, shoving her to the ground.

Rick has a gun raised and I run as fast as I can towards him, shouting for him to drop it. Laila's face is pressed against the concrete and I hate myself for not dealing with Rozzy sooner, but I had no idea she was this far off her rocker. I never listened to the voicemails or read her emails. I just pressed delete, thinking it would disappear.

But now I know that isn't how you deal with your problems in life. You need to face them head-on.

And now I will. Now and forever because it is Laila's life that is in jeopardy and I will never put her in this position again.

"Drop the gun," I say, praying that the police are on my heels, desperate to hear sirens in the distance.

"You lied to me, Colton. You said you loved me."

I step closer, wanting to calm her and her brother down long enough to get Laila out of here. But I see Rick's finger on the trigger. There isn't much time.

"Let her go," I say.

"Or what?" Rick spits.

"Shoot me instead."

"You don't mean that," Laila shouts.

"Yes, I do. Shoot me."

Just then, police cars pull into the parking lot, guns are raised. Rozzy is screaming, Rick is panicked, and I am goddamn terrified.

I know they won't stop until they get closer to their goal. That means Laila gone.

I dive for her just as a bullet pierces the night sky.

I land hard, covering the woman I love with my body, as a bloody flower blossoms on my chest. His gun falls to the gravel.

I press a hand to my heart, then look up and see that Laila has gotten a hold of the gun. She is standing, the revolver pointed to Rick.

She shoots him dead on, and he falls, and beside him, Rozzy is hysterical. Then she looks down at me, her eyes rimmed with red as the police officers run toward the crime scene.

"Laila," I cry, not wanting to die when I am so close to having what I want. A home with her.

She is shaking, falling to her knees, cradling me in her arms and I am begging for more time.

"I couldn't bring a child into this world

knowing a man like him was out there," she says.

I try to keep my eyes open as her words sink in.

"A child?"

"Yours," she whispers, pressing her lips to mine, giving me the oxygen I need to hold on for one more second. "We're having a baby."

"I love you, Laila," I whisper, my eyes refusing to stay open, fight as I might.

"Good, then don't go dying on me now."

She kisses me again, and then she takes my hand and presses it to her stomach. "I need you, Colton Miller. And so does your family."

I wake up in a hospital bed, groggy but alive.

"Oh, God," Laila cries, rushing toward me. "God, Colton, you scared me."

A doctor comes in and explains that I have been asleep for three days, following the surgery for the bullet wound. I narrowly escaped a fatal blow to the heart.

The nurses check my vitals, redress my bandages, and thankfully, the actual shot was clean. The actual wound is less than the size of a quarter, but the bandages are about six inches across. Once they are done making sure I'm okay, I look at the strongest woman I know. A fighter through and through, and braver than her petite frame would have you think. The mother of my child.

"Laila, I'm so sorry," I say, the memories from the parking lot flashing in my mind.

"Don't," she says. "No apologies. Just gratitude. Because Colton, we are here. Together. Against all odds."

"And Rick? Rozzy?"

Laila wipes the tears from her eyes. "He died. I killed him. And Rozzy is in jail."

"Oh, God, Laila," I say, as she crawls into the hospital bed. The doctor is shaking his head, but she doesn't care.

"I'll be careful but I just... I need to be with him."

"Did you tell him yet?" a nurse asks with a smile.

"Tell me what?" I ask.

Laila lifts her eyebrows and asks the nurse to hand her the pictures on the bedside table.

The nurse gives them to Laila, then pulls the curtain as she leaves, to give us privacy.

"It's kind of a big deal," she says.

"Bigger than what went down a few days ago?"

She twists her lips. "That was life or death. So, no, because this is only good news. At least, I think it is."

"Thank god, the last thing you need is another kidnapping."

She bites her lip, looking so damn beautiful when she does. "On the phone, when you mentioned the lakefront property to Rozzy, you were really speaking to me, weren't you?"

I nod. "I was hoping the words I was saying would give you hope, comfort, I prayed you would know they were for you, not her."

Laila nods. "I figured that out, and I was so overwhelmed, Colton. You hardly know me. I've been through so much, that's why I pushed you away. I was scared."

"I know, Laila. And it kills me that I didn't fight harder for you."

No," she says, shaking her head. "You were a real man. You listened when I said no. You respected me when I asked for space. You didn't bulldoze your way into my life and force me to be something I wasn't ready to be."

"But now?" I ask, my voice cracking. "Now, what are you ready for?"

She trembles as she looks into my eyes. "Now I'm ready for forever. And it's not just because I'm pregnant. It's because I love you. I knew the moment we met, but I was so terrified of being hurt. But now I know what true pain is-- being separated from you. Losing you. I want to build a life with you. A home. I want you to marry me, Colton Miller. I want to be your wife."

I'm speechless and amazed and goddamn in love.

"Get a nurse," I say.

Laila furrows her brows. "A nurse? Are you okay?"

"I just need a nurse, now."

Laila gets out of the bed and presses the nurse call button. A moment later the same nurse who had just been here arrives. "I need the pants I was wearing when I was brought in," I tell her.

"Pants?" Laila asks.

But I just nod and tell the nurse to hurry.

She does as I ask and a moment later she returns. "These?" she asks, handing me my jeans.

"Perfect." I take them from her and pull out the ring I had put in the pocket. "Laila, come back."

She steps toward me, the photos still in her hands.

I show her the ring, a twelve-carat diamond glittering in this fluorescently lit hospital room.

She gasps, shaking her head. "It's too much. It's..."

"Laila, I'm telling you, I could give you the world if you want it. But what I hope you want is my heart, plain and simple. I need you as my wife, my partner--my home."

She presses a hand to her mouth. "Before we commit, I have to show you something. I don't want you to think I tricked you into anything. And if you want to back out, you can. I understand. A lot of men would think of me as damaged goods. But I just--"

I cut her off. "Just show me, Laila."

She steps toward me and hands me the pictures. It takes me a moment to realize it is ultrasound images.

"Is this our baby?"

She shakes her head. "No. It's our babies."

I look closer, realizing there are arrows on the image, pointing to heartbeats.

I count them.

One. Two. Three. Four.

Four heartbeats.

"Quadruplets?" I ask, eyes widening at the shock and awe of the goddamn gift from above.

She nods. "It's kinda a package deal now."

"Hell yeah, it is. And I wouldn't have it any other way." Then I slip the ring on my bride's finger and pull her to me. "I love you, Laila, heart, and soul. Now let's get out of this hospital. We're homeward bound."

"Then we're already there," she says, her lips inches from mine. "Because when I'm with you, Colton, I'm right where I belong."

EPILOGUE 1

Laila

FIVE MONTHS LATER ...

oney doesn't buy happiness, but it does buy us a gorgeous lakefront home, custom built in less than five months flat. Jaxon's entire crew is hired, along with some stone workers from Spokane, electricians from Boise, and we hire Stella, Wilder's wife, to decorate the place.

In the end, this home is more than I could have ever imagined. I made Stella a Pinterest inspiration board in an effort to capture the vibe I was going for. Think bright and airy, peaceful and homey. Cherish laughed and said nothing was going to be peaceful once the babies come, and I'm sure she is right. But right now, all I care about is the fact this home Colton built for me is a safe place to raise my children.

It's more than I ever imagined for myself.

"You look so beautiful," Virginia says as she buttons the back of my wedding gown.

I roll my eyes. "I look huge."

"Not huge," Cherish laughs. "Just pregnant with four babies."

I look at myself in the full-length mirror. The three of us are in the master suite, and outside my home, the wedding guests are gathered. But I'm not thinking of any of them. I'm imagining the way Colton will look when he sees me dressed in white. His bride. His wife.

He has made it his duty to make sure I feel beautiful every day since we got engaged. He might promise to have and to hold me, but I have so many wounds from years of abuse. But now, when I look at myself in this white organza gown, I truly do feel lovely. I feel like I just might be the woman Colton sees. Colton's love has healed so many of my scars and allowed me to blossom into the woman I always wanted to become. Myself.

"Don't cry," Virginia says. "You'll ruin your makeup."

"I'm so emotional," I say, dabbing my eyes. "It must be the hormones."

Cherish places the veil on my head, the delicate tulle falling over my shoulders. "No, sweetie. It's not the hormones. It's love."

I pull my best friends into a tight embrace, my heart bursting with gratitude for having them here with me. I don't have extended family to stand with me today--but thankfully, we can choose our family. And I choose them.

Virginia looks at the time on her phone just as the wedding planner, Tilly, pops her head in the door. Outside there are a hundred people gathered, along with a photographer and a pastor. After we exchange our vows on the green lawn facing the lake, we will have a reception in a large tent on the property. Colton hired a wedding coordinator for us, and Tilly has planned this event down to every detail.

The fondant iced cake has four tiers, the parquet dance floor shines, and there is even a band set up for our first dance. It feels indulgent and opulent, but my friends have told me that life is hard. When you get blessings like this, you take them. And Colton isn't doing all this to show off. He's doing it because he wants me to feel like the queen he says I am.

"The ceremony is about to start," Tilly says. "You ready?"

"More than ready." And I mean it. I have experienced a lot of moments in my life when I felt weak and small. But as I walk outside with my bouquet of soft pink roses in hand, following in the footsteps of my bridesmaids Virginia and Cherish, I feel strong. And when I see Colton waiting for me at the end of the aisle I know I don't need to be strong on my own anymore. I have him to hold my hand, to lift me up.

When he takes my hand in his, a shiver of devotion runs up and down my spine. I want to make him happy for the rest of my life. And when he looks in my eyes and takes his vows, "Till death do us part" I know his words are true and real and promises he intends to keep.

When the pastor tells him to kiss his bride, he pulls me into his arms and I know without a shadow of a doubt he will never, ever let go.

"I love you, Mrs. Miller," he whispers in my ear.

My heart swells with emotion, I bite back the tears but he shakes his head. "Let them fall," he says. "Tears don't make you weak. They make you strong."

And he's right. I was so scared to give my heart to him, I pushed him away twice, even after I knew at first sight that he was the man for me. But tears are honest, they are a symbol of my vulnerability--with him and with everyone here. So, I don't wipe them away. I let them glisten on my cheeks, as a symbol of my love.

There are no guarantees in life, but there is

one thing I can hang onto. I can choose who I love, how wide and how deep.

And my love for Colton Miller is more expansive than this lake.

Hours later, he carries me over the threshold, and I laugh at the ridiculousness of it. I am much heavier than I was when we met, but he is stronger. His muscles even more ripped then they were when we met all those nights ago on the back porch. Colton has been working up a sweat every day since he moved to Miracle Mountain.

He's pounded in nails alongside Buck and Jaxon, framed the house with Wilder. He has carried in appliances with James and Hawk. He's installed windows with Beau and Bear. It's been a group effort and it has turned my fancy-pants movie star into a real mountain man.

"I am so ready to get you out of this dress, wife," he says as he sets me on the ground.

"Perfect. Because I'm desperate to get you inside of me." I give him a bright smile that is filled with all the memories of the day. Like when I tossed the bouquet and Virginia caught it. Or when Colton threw my garter belt, and Jonah's fingertips reached it first. I know more than one person looked at the pair of them with raised eyebrows.

"Oh, Laila," Colton groans, unbuttoning my dress. His fingertips graze over my skin with a gentleness that forces me to close my eyes, to lean back into his strong body.

"I love you, Colton," I whisper as my dress falls to the floor, as his hands cup my full breasts. My nipples are tight with expectation as he plucks them, as he plants kisses down my neck, sending a thrill of excitement over my body.

"You are the most beautiful bride," he tells me, and I turn to him, my big belly between us, his hard cock now in my hand.

"Thank you for fighting for me. For not giving up on me," I say, as he pulls me to the bed, as he leans over me. As his length enters me with decision and desire.

"I will always be here for you; for our babies," he says, his eyes on mine and my body opening up to him all over again. He feels so good and so right, and as we begin rocking against one another, our bodies in sync and our minds one, I know that we've been homeward bound since the moment we met. And now and forever, here we are.

Right where we belong.

Chapter Seventeen

EPILOGUE 2

Colton

EIGHT MONTHS LATER...

When her water breaks, it's as dramatic as it seems in the movies. She's in the kitchen, eating spoonfuls straight from the pint of ice cream, barefoot, and so very pregnant.

"I'm not ready," she moans. "It wasn't supposed to break at home."

Carrying quads has meant we are a high-risk pregnancy, and the C-section is scheduled in three days. No one was thinking her water would break before then.

"It's okay, love," I tell her, rushing to her side. My fingers already pressing send on a call to the doctor. Within minutes, there is a plan, a helicopter is on its way, so we can get to the Boise State hospital within the hour.

"I'm scared, Cole. I don't know how to do this," she whimpers as a contraction washes over her. I hate seeing her in so much pain. It kills me to watch, but I know she needs me to be her rock, so I take her hand, let her squeeze it until I think the bones might break, and lead her to the front porch.

"I'm right here, Laila. We will be with the doctor soon, and then you can meet your babies." I don't know if it's the right words, but I am doing my best to be the man she needs. "You're so close, mama."

She looks at me with tears in her eyes. "I want to be a good mom, Colton. I never had one and I'm scared I'm gonna mess up."

"Shh," I say, kissing her forehead, as the helicopters' loud propellers signal its impending arrival. "You are going to be the best mom these babies could ask for," I assure her, believing it with all that I am. All that I could be.

"How do you know? Because I'm not as sure," she says, putting words to her deepest fear. That she isn't enough.

I take her face in hands, looking deeply into her eyes. "Love is a choice. And you choose them. Love is what they need, and you will offer it in spades."

I kiss her then, knowing soon it will no longer be just her and me. Our lives are changing today.

"I love you, Laila. Now let's go do the damn thing."

She laughs through her tears, and I'm glad. Heaven knows there will be enough screaming soon enough. Giving birth to four babies is no easy feat. We know there will be two boys and two girls. We spent the last several months choosing their names.

We decided on names that all mean blessing or miracle. After all, we are living in the valley of Miracle Mountain. The girls are Beatrix and Dorothy (nicknamed Dottie) and the boys are Asher and Bennett. I cannot wait to see them, hold them, inhale their new baby smell. God, I've become a sap--but how could I not? I'm a father now, and the luckiest man this mountain has ever seen.

"You are gonna look so sexy wearing your babies in a sling, you know that, don't you Colton? The press is gonna die," Laila says as the helicopter lands on our private pad. A photo shoot is scheduled in two weeks at the house with *People* magazine getting the exclusive.

The hospital bag is on the porch and my wife's hands are in mine. We are ready as the medics run toward us.

She may be a small town girl, but we are still very much in the limelight. It's an honor to be an actor, to have the job that I do, and it isn't something I take lightly. I went on a road trip searching for a way out, but I found my way home. I didn't need to leave acting, I just needed to leave Hollywood.

Now, I'm committed to bringing more stories of love and redemption to the big screen. After I won an Oscar for the role I played as Luke in the movie I filmed in Linesworth, *Heartbreak Mountain*, and Laila was my date for the ceremony, we became America's sweetheart couple.

At that moment, Laila and I agreed that we would invite the public to see parts of our lives because the world can use more love stories. There is no such thing as too many happily ever afters.

And this one?

It's just about perfect.

There is nothing quite as good as coming home sweet home.

I hope you loved your trip to Miracle Mountain!
It's my favorite place to travel and I'm so

happy that so many readers have found a place for themselves here, too.

I am just finishing up the next book in the series and I am sooo excited for it.
It's about a mountain man widower with six kids ... Let's hope he finds what he is looking for on this mountain!
It's gonna be a tear-jerker!

Coming Late 2018:
RAISED: The Mountain Man's Babies
Book 9

I came to this mountain to move on.
I've been through enough, and so have my six
kids.
They deserve a Christmas with new memories.

When I find a rental house that's big enough for my brood, that comes with a live in cook, it feels too good to be true.

It's an undertaking, but the owner Virginia doesn't flinch. She's a beautiful woman who has seen hard times.

With a gentle ease about her and a depth I long to reach — I know I've found more than my equal.

I've found my Christmas miracle.

But when my oldest daughter takes her teenage rebellion one step too far, it threatens an avalanche on this mountain.

Dear Reader,

No need to put on your mittens and parka. We're not hiking up the snow-capped peaks this Christmas. Just open that kindle and let the newest man on Miracle Mountain decide if you've been naughty or nice.

xo, frankie

Download: RAISED

Frankie Love writes filthy-sweet stories about bad boys and mountain men.

As a thirty-something mom who is ridiculously in love with her own bearded hottie, she believes in love-at-first-sight and happily-ever-afters.

She also believes in the power of a quickie.

Find Frankie here:
www.frankielove.net

www.ingramcontent.com/pod-product-compliance
Lightning Source LLC
Chambersburg PA
CBHW031303060726
47590CB00003B/1038